I0637841

After Dinner Conversation Themes
Crimes & Punishments Edition

Philosophy | Ethics Short Story Fiction

After Dinner Conversation *Themes* – Crimes & Punishments

After Dinner Conversation publishes fictional stories that explore ethical and philosophical questions in an informal manner. The purpose of these stories is to generate thoughtful discussion in an open and easily accessible manner.

Names, characters, businesses, organizations, places, events, and incidents are either the product of the author's imagination or are used fictitiously. Any resemblance to actual persons, living or dead, events, or locales is entirely coincidental. This book is published in print and electronic format.

ISBN 979-8-9896194-2-9
Library of Congress Control Number: 2023952668

.

Editor in Chief: *Kolby Granville*
Edition Editor: *Kolby Granville*
Story Editor: *R.K.H. Ndong*
Copy Editor: *Kate Bocassi*
Cover Design: *Shawn Winchester*
Design, layout, and discussion questions by After Dinner Conversation.

https://www.afterdinnerconversation.com

After Dinner Conversation believes humanity is improved by ethics and morals grounded in philosophical truth and that philosophical truth is discovered through intentional reflection and respectful debate. In order to facilitate that process, we have created a growing series of short stories across genres, a monthly magazine, and two podcasts. These accessible examples of abstract ethical and philosophical ideas are intended to draw out deeper discussions with friends, family, and students.

Table Of Contents

* * *

From the Editor

Of course, the short stories in our monthly magazine are intended to be used in classrooms, so it was no surprise when we got an email from another professor asking for permission to make copies for his class. What was unique was he wanted to make copies of <u>ten</u> stories for his class, all related to a single topic. And, the idea for this series was born.

Why not group stories from our back catalog by theme and sell them as books for classrooms? So, we did a request for proposals, and received a huge response from professor wanting to pick and create themed books. We selected the very best and starting working with teachers to assemble themed books. AI Ethics, Medical Ethics, Government Ethics, etc.

I opted to keep this themed book on punishment for myself, picking the stories from our back catalog. I've always found one of humanity's most basic and fascinating questions to be, "Is the goal of punishment to stop crime, or do justice?"

I think you'll find these stories run the spectrum of opportunities for discussion, so if one story isn't your cup of tea, keep reading. The next will be on an entirely different aspect of the nature of crimes and punishments.

Happy reading to you, the friends/loved ones you share stories with, or the classroom you teach. I'm sure you'll find wonderful springboards within the bounds of this book for thoughtful conversation. Dedicated to my sister.

Kolby Granville – Editor

Idle Horns

Garrett Davis

* * *

The tongs feel heavy in Bub's clawed hands. Seven millennia without incident and he freezes during inspection. In front of Bub, is a thief? He's bound by thick rope to an office chair with poor lumbar support. Bub had truly thought of everything. *So why am I nervous?* He smiles apologetically at the overseer who'd come to witness today's punishments; one of the original angels who fell alongside the great beast. He motions for Bub to continue. The thief senses the change too. Hope glimmers, a gold mist, rises off him like steam. Bub shakily reaches out with the tongs and clamps onto the thief's toe nail. His feet are bare and bloody. They were already on the fourth little piggy. Six left—sixteen if he does the hands for extra credit. Bub likes counting. He enjoys the steady progression and the satisfaction of meeting a quota. Bub pulls. There's resistance at first, but then it comes free. He drops it in the bucket with the others. The overseer nods approvingly, and Bub forgets all about the sudden wave of nausea and is quite sure of his place in the natural order of things.

Until pitchfork day, four thousand years later.

Bub and his fellow devils of the fourth circle stand on the fields of ruin. It is here that much of the bedrock blasted from the ninth circle into the atmosphere fell back to Tartarus. Altars had been hewn from the stones, and it is here that they tied their sinners. Bub sharpens the tines of his pitchfork slowly, methodically. Flashing a fanged grin at his victim, Bub realizes that the man he is preparing to run through just so happens to be the exact same thief from inspection day! Glancing around his stone, Bub sees his coworkers are engrossed in their work. Sulphur and screams fill the air. No one pays him any attention. Everyone loves pitchfork day. Bub launches forward and does something he's never done before. He asks the sinner what he's done to deserve such a punishment. What the man says haunts Bub forever.

He says, "Ye-Aaaarrrg!"

Pulling the pitchfork free, Bub slaps the man across the cheek until he regains his senses. "Oh, don't be such a baby. Tell me why you are here?"

"Bikes!" the man says.

"Bikes?"

"Yes bikes. I—I stole bikes and sold them."

"How many?"

The thief's sweating, ash-stained brow furrows, "Sir?"

"How many bikes did you steal? Two? Four? Six?"

The thief's face contorts in what is either great pain or deep thought. "Um, well I'm not sure. Maybe a dozen. Look I'm really sorry—"

Bub plunges the farm tool into the man once more, but

his heart is no longer in it. The fourth circle suddenly seems cold. *How long can one maim the souls of the damned and still get something out of it?* he thinks. Bub steps back to watch his brethren do their foul work. Amidst the screams and blood and gore, he recognizes them for what they are—animals driven by bloodlust compelled to torture without end. *All this torture and pain, all because someone stole twelve bikes four thousand years ago?* How trivial. A drop in the ocean of eternity. How meaningless forever suddenly became in the face of a dozen bicycles. So Bub does what, to his knowledge, no one in hell has ever done.

Bub quits.

The pitchfork clatters at his clawed feet. Walking over to the immense wall of the pit he begins to climb. He doesn't look back, only up, using the sky as his target. A sickly yellow bull's eye far, far above. Eventually his broken and bleeding hands crest the edge of the cliff and he feels something soft. Bub pulls himself up onto the plains of limbo and up a small grassy knoll the color of antique slate. Chest heaving, he watches a tenebrous geyser of ash spew from the pit he left behind and up into the atmosphere. It falls back to the plains like snow, suffocating plant life where it piles. Next to him on the knoll a sapling struggles to push free of the soot.

Digging it out, Bub asks it, "Well, what now?"

The plant says nothing of course, but silence seems a profound answer. Someone will come to fetch him eventually. When they get around to it. *That's the problem with eternity*, he thinks. It's *a woefully long time—all of it, in fact.* They might not notice he's gone for thousands of years. Bub yawns and shuts his eyes. When he opens them again, the sapling has grown into a tree. Its roots have wound their way around his body ensnaring him while he had slept. Bub shrugs. This spot seems as good as any for a holiday. There is nowhere else he can flee to. Earth is strictly for the mortals, and as for Heaven... Well, he knows *that* ship sailed long ago.

Resolving to enjoy his time off, Bub lounges and lays, loafs and dawdles and becomes quite adept at dozing off. Apart from these "rigorous" activities, Bub counts. He tallies the hairs on his head. Quantifies the tentacles on a passing nightmare and adds up the very circles of hell: one hundred thousand, thirty-two and nine, respectively.

A monster slowly floats into view, wafting up over the cliff edge like ash. A living paradox, the monster is humanoid with barbarian musculature but possesses cunning eyes. Both beautiful and terrible to behold, his youthful body exudes an aura of decay. Bub counts the wings. There are four. Two tiny wings growing from his head and two sprouting from the ankles. They hang limply in the air as if they are merely decorative. He wields a very impractical weapon: a golden staff wrapped with two live cobras, each vying to strike the killing blow onto the other. Fresh blood trickles down its haft informing Bub of its ornamental nature.

An Antediluvian of the Sixth Circle had been sent to pursue him. Bub shrinks down into the roots, willing them to pull him into the soil. A team of Imps or Succubi, minor demons like himself would have been more practical—but to send a mighty Antediluvian—apparently an example was to be made. Landing softly, the Antediluvian scans the surrounding hills for his quarry. Black eyes fall on the tree, and he marches in its direction. Bub writhes against his bonds but is unable to free himself in time. The Antediluvian looms above. Bub raises a hand to block an incoming blow that never arrives. Peeking through his fingers, Bub watches his pursuer use the staff's unornamented end to rip roots free of the ground.

"Been looking for you for ages. Glad to have the job done. Right! Get to your feet and we'll be off. Weather is quite pleasant up here. Can see why you picked it. Should've looked here first, really. All that wasted time. Can't imagine climbing though, but then I've got these little suckers." The Antediluvian clicks his ankles together causing the wings to flutter excitedly.

Bub opens his mouth three times to speak but stammers so badly he has to regroup and start over. The truth is that he hadn't expected such a fearsome demon to have such a light and airy voice. Or speak in such a rapid-fire way. Seemingly as fast as the creature's tongue would allow. There is also something vaguely familiar about him.

"You—you're Hermes, aren't you?" Bub asks.

"Did the scepter gave it away?"

"The wings, actually," Bub says. "Aren't they supposed to be on your hat?"

"Aha! Got you there. The hat hides them. Usually it's this old thing gives me away." He shakes the staff back and forth producing annoyed hisses from the entwined reptiles. "Don't know why I keep it. I'm sentimental, I guess. Enough chitchat. Time's a wasting, and people want to talk to you."

"Are you always the messenger?" Bub asks.

"I dabble here and there, but in answer: Yes, for the most part. Call me Merc by the way. Shorter saves time."

He extends a hand for Bub to shake, who does so cautiously. Merc uses the handshake to pull Bub to his feet. Bub flinches as Merc brushes the remaining ash off his shoulders.

Merc seems to bear no cruel intention. This lack of malice unsettles Bub, but it also gives him an idea. "So you found me. What now?"

"Take you down to the ninth, and then I'm off to the next job."

The ninth, deepest circle of hell, reserved for the treacherous and ruled by the Morning Star himself. Brood mothers often tell Fledglings tales, in order to give them nightmares, about how all nine circles are in reality the impact crater from the beast's fall. So hot is the fire of the black lake that the ash rides thermals all the way up to the plains of limbo. Chained to its surface: Lucifer enemy of creation, and he wants to speak to Bub.

"The ninth!" Bub says, feeling suddenly weak in the knees.

Merc makes the whistling sound of a dropping bomb. "Straight to the bottom."

"Look you don't *have* to take me anywhere. No one *has* to do anything. It's all pointless."

"Good," Merc says. "We've agreed this is pointless. Let's go."

"Wait," Bub says. "You're not listening. Say I stole twelve bikes—"

"Bikes?"

"Yes, bikes. But it doesn't matter it could be adultery or murder too. If you compare that one time—"

"Or twelve—"

"Shut up!" Bub interrupts. "Think of existence as a whole rather than life and afterlife. Over ten years, you steal bikes and then get tortured for ten times the ninth power for it. The punishment is disproportionate to the crime, and yet those ten years are being held up as more important than the rest."

Merc frowns. "That does seem a tad unfair. What do you propose I do then?"

"Don't take me back," Bub says. "Tell them you couldn't find me. Or stay here. You said it yourself the weather is good."

"Here?" Merc rubs his chin. "What would we do? What have you been doing?"

"Nothing," Bub shrugs. "It's actually really nice."

Merc shakes his head as though a chill has run up his spine. "No, no, no, no. Always something to be done. Cows to steal, souls to carry, people to trick. I'd simply die of boredom. Now come along."

Merc grabs Bub by the arm and pulls him towards the edge of the pit. Bub can feel the heat of the thermals, hear the screams of the punished, and he does not want to go back. One last idea comes to him, and it is strong enough that some hope glimmers off his skin. Any fight against Merc, a Sixth ringer and a very old god, will not go Bub's way. But being a god might also be Merc's weakness. Monotheistic religions won out against the old pantheons not because the latter lost its believers but because the former consolidated all its power into one being. The old gods, gods like Merc, segregated and took dominion of specific realms and attributes. Merc didn't seem the type to put up with nonsense, so Bub goes limp and falls to the ground. Merc stumbles at the sudden lack of resistance.

"Get up! Get up!" Merc yells, stamping his feet.

Bub does not reply. He lies face down in the grass breathing deep of its earthen musk in case he never gets another chance. Merc kicks him with a winged foot. Bub grunts but does his best to stay still. He counts the blades of grass. If he fails to comply and engages in passive resistance, Merc might just get bored, cut his losses, and return to report his whereabouts to his superiors, giving Bub the chance to hide once more.

Merc swings with his scepter which lands with a thunk! The snakes, quick as lightning, bite in the brief instant of contact. Years of torturing has taught Bub not to scream. Screams encourage the attacker. There are six hundred sixty-seven blades of grass in his field of vision. One less and he would have taken it as an omen.

"Enough!" Merc says.

It worked. I've won.

Merc slams his staff in the soft earth near Bub's face. A pulse of power radiates out from the staff and into the surrounding landscape. The ground trembles and there's a telltale lurch in Bub's stomach as the ground falls out from under him. The entire hillside crumbles into the yawning emptiness of the pit below. Merc hovers in place and whistles the unmistakable note of a bomb being dropped.

Bub falls, smote by a god he does not recognize. Air, full of ash and the smell of brimstone, howls in his ears to the point where he cannot hear his own screams. He watches the yellow sky recede to be a dot the size of his thumbnail, only to get smaller still. It feels as though he's being slurped up like a plate of entrails, sliding ever closer to some dreadful maw. He shoots past his former home on the fourth circle and wonders if anyone there witnesses his passing. The air gets hotter. Miniature bolts of lightning lick at exposed skin, leaving black scorch marks where they touch. To his knowledge, he is the only demon in all of eternity to quit, but he knows he is not the first to make this headlong plunge. Mortals and monsters alike often forget that Satan was once the angel at God's right hand. *Why wouldn't they?* Satan spent far less time being that man. And yet he's defined by that act of rebellion. Was he the devil while he fell? Is he an angel now? Just who will Bub meet at the bottom?

The force of gravity is overwhelming. Bub feels like he's stretching, as if his face is falling faster than his feet. The nausea-inducing lurch in his stomach does not fade but instead intensifies. He passes the fifth circle, rockets through the sixth. Seven is alight with flame, but the ninth is a blackest ball of obsidian, growing steadily larger as he plummets through the eighth. The impact does not send ash streaming to the sky far, far above. It doesn't break ground, adding a tenth layer to hell, but it does break him. Any eternal being cannot be created or destroyed. Perhaps this is why, God did not simply will Lucifer into the nothingness from whence he came. But instead, like Merc, he was repurposed. Bub is a conscious pile of flesh and shattered bone. With nothing intact for the muscles to pull on, he's immobile. He can however see out of one intact eye, left miraculously undamaged. A miracle that has him praying to go blind.

Chunks of flaming tree crash down around him. Its kindling illuminates his surroundings. There are four impossibly large lengths of silver chain secured by four identical golden spikes driven into the obsidian bedrock. Bound by these great chains is a giant. He's stretched out over a section of the black rock that wobbles like gelatin. Its thin crust ruptures, spewing forth white hot magma onto the giant's back. He grimaces in pain, and Bub notices all thirty-two teeth have been ground down to little more than nubs.

A smaller man kneels down to inspect what is left of Bub.

He's wearing a three-piece suit designed in Earth fashion. His hair is neatly combed and parted. Resting on his nose is a pair of gold-rimmed spectacles with tinted red glass. He pinches Bub's flesh and rubs it between two fingers the way a toddler might play with a booger. Bub's tongue rolls in an empty cavity that had once been his mouth. The shrapnel of his bones grind against his soft tissues under the stranger's red-tinted gaze.

"You're Bub," the stranger says.

With no mouth, Bub cannot answer—cannot scream.

"It's okay. I know you can't answer. Think it in your mind."

Yes.

"Good," the man says. "Do you know who I am?"

Yes, but how—

"That's the body," Lucifer says tilting his head in the direction of the giant. "Think of me as the unholy spirit if that makes it easier." He pauses. "You quit."

Yes

"Why?"

Bikes.

"Bikes?"

Bub rolls his remaining eyeball, painful but satisfying nonetheless. Bub recalls the thief four thousand years ago and walks this unholy spirit through his revelations and actions up until this moment. *Can you convince someone who sees himself as greater than God, that he had been wrong all along?* Bub wonders. Then tries to un-wonder it. Lucifer takes off his glasses and polishes them on the fine fabric of his vest. He appears to be at least considering the possibility. Then with a sigh, he places them back onto his face.

"You mistake me," he quietly says. "I do not dole out punishment for a sin committed. I do not sit and judge. It is not about a moment set next to eternity, but ownership of that moment for it. I do what I do not to punish mortals but to see the pain inflicted on the face of God when I sully something he loves, and to that end I use you."

The giant rattles its chain as a fresh burst of magma sears its back. The cacophony of metal echoes ad nauseam through the caverns of the ninth circle. Lucifer wrinkles his nose. "Oh, quit your whining!" He turns back to Bub. "If I cannot use you in my war effort," he says, pinching a bit of Bub's skin and stretching it, "and let's be honest for once, I can't." He lets go, and the flesh droops back into a saggy pile. "Then I shall punish that idleness."

Lucifer stands up, pulling a handkerchief from his breast pocket and wipes his hands clean of some perceived filth. At the same time, hands sprout from the ground around Bub. They knead and massage skin, working the muscle against the grit of bone. There is nothing he can do but count to infinity. He starts at one.

* * *

This story first appeared in the After Dinner Conversation—September 2020 issue.

Discussion Questions

1. Bub says, "All this torture and pain, all because someone stole twelve bikes four thousand years ago? How trivial a drop in the ocean of eternity." Is the concept of eternal punishment for any individual sin ever just? Is the problem simply that we see bike theft as a "minor sin," but God does not?
2. For what, if any, actions would eternal punishment ever be just?
3. Do you believe there is a "hell?" If so, what is it like and what would be the reasons for someone to be sent to it?
4. Is it fair that Bub is being punished for eternity for *refusing* to punish people for eternity?
5. Why is there a hell at all? If God is all-knowing, and all-powerful, and all good, how is it even possible for a person to sin?

* * *

Community of Peers

Dean Gessie

* * *

After the war, I travelled to a village in the south of the province. It was my intention to vacation for the weekend in an unknown land. I followed a small river that was alternately green beneath the foliage of the forest and blue while it coursed through elevated plains and sunken but exposed valleys. I was driving one of those all-terrain vehicles that permitted me to follow paths that were clearly less travelled. It was not an aquatic vehicle, however, and an error in judgment forced me to abandon it to a finely camouflaged bog. I breast-stroked to safety while my truck took water through its sunroof.

With mischance at my back, I followed the river on foot until it opened up into a small lake. On the northern-most shore of the lake, a settlement, of sorts, sprawled upward into black hills, its watery threshold flagged and dotted with light, fishing craft. I walked through vineyards and a peach orchard, each of these bursting with fruit, until I came to what appeared to be the main thoroughfare of the village.

The street was desolate save for mongrels as numerous as flies. They lounged about on their flabby bellies, yawning and blinking in the sun, and, apparently, abandoned by their lords and masters. One of the mongrels, more animated than the rest, fell in behind me wagging its short, stubby tail. I stopped to pet its flank and noticed that its tail had been freshly severed at its point. Remarkably, when the dog craned its long neck to look, as a greyhound might or a horse, the root of its tail became fixed when I clutched the memory of its remainder.

I had little time to contemplate the peculiar psychology of the bitch at my calves. Out of the silence of this place came a young boy running as fast as his legs would take him, huffing and puffing dramatically. I gestured with my arms, like a traffic cop, for him to stop. I would have thought the gesture clear enough to communicate my needs, but the boy sped past me as though my existence were in question, his thin, eager face flushed with purpose and exertion.

I followed with some speed and anxiousness of my own until I saw the lad disappear into a throng of people whose focus elsewhere precluded my seeing their faces. The crowd before me, the emptiness of the village, was mingling about a large and dead tree whose stark grey branches thrust skyward like an ancient hand contorted to hold a crystal ball. There looked to be a hundred or so gathered and they were dressed in the traditional garments of country folk. This struck me as odd since my travels during the war had revealed to me the penetration of the global clothing market.

On tiptoe, I noticed that there was a man of about thirty tied to the tree, his arms pulled back and around the trunk of it, his hands bound, his head bowed. A two-wheel, wooden cart balanced on long wooden posts stood some five feet to the left of him, its carriage filled with stones.

To confirm my suspicions, I inquired of an elderly gentleman as to the nature of the gathering. The man did not answer my question, but regarded me with astonishment, his nose hairs disentangling and vibrating with each shallow and rapid exhalation. He then proceeded to push his way into the crowd until he broke into the clearing that separated the gathering from its victim. He conferred with a lean, tall gentleman who appeared to be the arbiter of the ceremony and pointed excitedly in my direction. All eyes turned toward me, sized me head to toe. My existence was no longer in question.

The tall man, whom I learned later to be the village mayor, invited me forward with his hand. I and my dog heeded his invitation and walked the corridor made for us by the separating throng.

"You are a stranger?" asked the man.

The question was asinine since the mayor of this small town would surely know better. However, the emotional content in the man's voice was that of a lottery winner overwhelmed by the evidence.

"Yes," I said.

"You have come at an opportune time," he said. "We are about to execute a man."

It was as I suspected. I asked the fellow why, however, the time should be described as opportune.

"Our people have a custom," he said. "If there is a stranger among us, he is given the honor of casting the first stone. It is our way of including him in the life of the village. It is our way of extending the boundaries of justice, of communicating justice between the communities of the earth."

I congratulated the mayor on the lofty goals of his citizens. Most public officials concern themselves with more modest matters, I said, like keeping drug addicts and hookers off the street. And so it was that I was to represent the cohabitation of time and space with the laws of men. For both sundry and weighty reasons, I queried the crimes of the condemned man.

"For that," said the man, "you will have to trust us. He has been found guilty by due process in a court of his peers. The evidence was overwhelming and indisputable."

I did not betray a smirk, but I had seen more than once overwhelming and indisputable evidence tumble like a house of cards. As a result, I expressed some reticence about firing a death blow under these conditions.

The mayor appeared dismayed that I was making a debate of it, that I wouldn't credit the wisdom of his particular collective.

"Where you are from," he said, "are there executions?"

I assured him that my country took great pleasure in extinguishing the lives of criminals.

"And is your reticence as great when men and women are killed and you have no knowledge of or interest in their crimes?"

I informed the man, as he no doubt wished and anticipated, that I had long ago handed over the responsibility for such decisions and actions.

"Precisely," he said. "You trust others to end the lives of others on your behalf. You tacitly condone their judgments with your indifference and weave the thread of the noose. Will you not trust us this one time and exercise the sovereignty of your will?"

I congratulated the mayor on the quality of his argument, so compelling was it that I felt as though I were on trial as much as the condemned man had been.

"You needn't do it," said the mayor. "It's your free choice to assist or stand aside."

The mayor saw my self-conflict, how my mental processes were virtually stalled, like a large machine creaking inexorably to a halt.

"Are you a baseball player?" he asked.

"No," I said, "I don't have the legs for it. But," I added, "I have been to the fair often and won many prizes for female companions by striking the effigy of a clown's face with a rubber ball."

"Good," he said. "You have both the power and the ability to end the life of this criminal quickly or, at the very least, knock him unconscious so that the cleaning up is less painful for all concerned. I will tell you this," he added. "The women with children will cast the first stones, if you choose not to."

We returned to the front of the gathering. The women in our midst collected their stones from the two-wheel cart. I was provided a large, almost perfectly spherical stone.

I felt my adopted dog, the short-haired mongrel from the street, weaving its way playfully between my legs. I knew that no one could see the lost half of its tail but that she, herself, reacted to its absence. It was the invisibility of this impregnable reality that permitted us ignorance of its existence. It occurred to me that the phantom limb—that which we have cut away and discarded—was summation to the mayor's argument.

I was only disposed to a ten-foot buffer between myself and the criminal. I fired the stone, shaped very much like a ball, with as much force and accuracy as I could muster. It struck him flush mid-temple. The breaking of his skull would be sickening to some. A blue, bloody bruise emerged in relief.

The women around me tossed their stones, joylessly, to the ground. They were prepared to do as much but the feeling seemed to be that I had managed the work efficiently.

The crowd dispersed and returned in the direction of the village. In one breath, the mayor informed me that the deceased criminal had raped a young girl and that he would be cut down and buried. His soft smile communicated satisfaction with me and, by extension, satisfaction with himself. "We will surface your vehicle from the water bog," he said. "You are a free man."

Notwithstanding the objective execution of what I had done, the seeming incontrovertibility of my decision and the groundwork of judgment, the criminal's face, at the moment that I threw the stone, appeared to my eyes as that of a clown.

I hadn't done anything extraordinary.

* * *

This story first appeared in the After Dinner Conversation—February 2021 issue.

Discussion Questions

1. What is your opinion of the narrator for choosing to throw the stone at the end of the story? Do you judge him, or is the choice to throw/not throw a personal one?

2. Would you throw the stone? Is there additional information you would want to know prior to making your decision?

3. Would your decision change if the prisoner was going to be set free if you refused? What if the local custom was to keep the person in solitary confinement and torture them until a foreigner came to kill them? Would you then be okay with a "mercy" killing?

4. Does it matter that the penalty is death? What if the punishment were something severe, but less harsh? Would you then agree to give out the punishment?

5. Are there "universal morals" you believe the village is not following or are all laws simply the codification of cultural norms?

6. Would your decision change if you didn't find their "trial" system to be valid in your opinion? (*E.g. They put a rock in water and guilt/innocence was based on if it floated.*)

* * *

Form Seven Alpha

Richard Pettigrew

* * *

So here I sit with it again, Form 7α. It is printed on cheap paper with low-quality ink that smudges under my fingers. The option they judge least bad for me has been scored through, unavailable, while the four other options remain. Since the last time I faced this choice, they've updated the logo for whatever committee it is that processes these things. I sit with the cracked rubber stamp and the grimy pad of red ink. When I press the stamp into the ink and then onto the form, it will read "REQUESTED." So, which punishment should I request this time?

* * *

The last time I had to complete Form 7α was a decade ago. It was my first time, and I was a different person. Two days before, I'd arrived to visit my sister, who lives on a different island from me, separated from mine by the lush, teeming forest. I crossed at night. There was me, nine other travelers, and a guide. The crossing was legal. The guide was state-approved and carried her Form 5ρ, which bore the stamp of the relevant committees. The timing was optimum, four hours after sundown, when all but two of the forest's species were asleep, and our footsteps would disturb the ecosystem minimally. The problem was me. I was illegal.

The islands were established fifty years ago. Three are residential clearings, each a thousand acres, where we live our day-to-day lives. Three are correctional clearings, only ten acres each, where we undertake any necessary punishments. Six islands in a sea of forest that totals six billion acres.

The original authorities determined that each citizen may cross from their home island to one of the other residential islands and back again at most once per year. Even this was a compromise with those who had argued there should be no crossings at any time and for any reason. We must impinge no further on the forest, they said. It must remain inviolate. But that view did not prevail. It transpires there are limits to our ecological purity. Instead, between any two islands, ten people may cross with a guide each night.

That night, I was one of the ten. The problem was that I'd already crossed that year, only two months before, in fact. That time, like this time, it was to see my sister.

* * *

She's six years older than I am, and ever since I can remember, she's been the sun in my life. Every story from my childhood has her at its center: something funny she said, some game she invented, something perfect she did.

I always knew she carried a burden. Every four or five years, sometimes for months on end, a shadow would fall over her. The light would go from her eyes, the cadence from her voice, and there would be a flatness to everything she did. Part of me dreaded those months, but another part that I hated in myself welcomed them. She'd spend more time at home, more time with me, and I'd read to her late into the night.

Our mother said they'd have called it depression when she was young, but now that word means only a dip in the ground, a hollow in the earth. Our mother said they'd have given her medicine for her depression in the old world. But it wasn't talked of now—these sicknesses that show up in your mind rather than your body. We were supposed to have left them behind when we moved to the islands. They were born of a cosmic unease, they said, an unconscious, ever-present guilt about how we'd been treating the land and its creatures. They assured us this would lift when we started to live ecologically within our means, when we made our peace with the earth. But of course, it didn't. And now we had no way to talk about what my sister suffered and no way to get her any help.

Her latest bout had started as the dry season began in June. I'd sensed it approaching during our phone calls and in her letters. As soon as I was certain, I requested leave from work, telling them my sister had tripped and fallen and broken both wrists and needed help at home. They granted me two weeks, and I made the crossing the next night, my first crossing that year, all perfectly legal.

For two weeks, I read to her in the shade of an acacia tree that grew outside her living block. Always the books our mother had left for us—stories from her own childhood of things we'd never seen, like airplanes and plastic toys, telephones that you could carry in your pocket, and creatures like small black and white jaguars who would live with you in your rooms. I knew that nothing I did would shorten my sister's suffering, but perhaps my presence might temper her despair a little.

When I left, we both cried. When I returned to my island, I felt helpless. Every evening, I'd call her, but she'd say little, so I'd read to her some more. We were fast running out of stories from our mother's books. Over time, she said less and less.

I didn't know anyone in her living block. I'm certain she's popular there; she's been popular everywhere she's ever been. But no one called around when I was visiting. These things, it's understood, are kept within a family.

So when, two months after my visit, my sister stopped speaking at all on the phone and then stopped even answering, I knew I had to get back to her. But it was only August. I couldn't cross legally again until June of the following year. On the islands, years begin with the start of the dry season and end as the flood season recedes. Two seasons in each year, and I'd made my single permitted crossing for that year right at the beginning of the first.

So I stole my neighbor's identity card, made my application in his name, and received approval to cross two nights later. I couldn't request more leave from work, so I knew I could be there for only two days between shifts. Nonetheless, I had to go.

* * *

The night of the crossing, the sky was clear, the moon was bright, and the heat of the day rose away from the earth. At the gate before we left, the guards checked our backpacks and handed us the headlamps we would use for the crossing. We were allowed no food while we were in the forest because it might attract the creatures, and only water to drink. The red lights of the headlamps would let us pass with minimal disturbance. The theater of our ecological sensitivity is elaborate.

Once through the checkpoint and into the forest, the path we trod was a narrow, precise groove through the stacks of moss-covered branches and piles of leaf mulch that carpeted the ground. Occasionally, our headlamps would illuminate a tree trunk that had fallen across the path during the day. If it were small enough, the guide would carefully move it to the side; if it were too large for that, we'd have to clamber over, our hands and our feet slipping on its smooth bark, which was damp from the humidity.

We walked in single file. An elderly gentleman who walked in front of me stumbled more than once, and I took his arm to steady him and reassured him silently. He nodded briefly in acknowledgment.

During long straight stretches of path, when I didn't have to concentrate on keeping my footing, my mind wandered, and I felt what I had always felt in the forest. An inexplicable urge rose in me to run off the track, deep into the tangle of ferns, and find a glade among the trees and lie perfectly still in the moonlight. Maybe my sister could come to join me there, and I could read to her as we grew old. Her depression would lift, and the light would return to her eyes. She'd invent games for us to play under the moonlight, and even now, as adults, we'd find the joy in them we found as children.

The crossing took six hours, and I wondered at times whether the elderly man ahead of me would make it. We weren't allowed to speak on the crossings, lest we should draw attention to our presence, so I couldn't learn why he was risking the journey. The authorities make very clear that these expeditions are undertaken at your own risk. They will never authorize a rescue team or send medical assistance. Only once, I'd heard, had anyone failed to complete a crossing. They were left, as promised, and only nine showed up at the gate of the receiving island that night. The following night, as people crossed that route in reverse, the body was gone, swallowed by the forest and its creatures.

As we reached the gate of my sister's island, the trees cleared, and the moon lit up our little band of exhausted travelers. There was a small cluster of people waiting to welcome us. An elderly man in a long white tunic waited to greet the man who'd been stumbling ahead of me. I watched as they embraced, and tears filled their eyes. My sister, of course, was not there, but I hadn't expected she would be.

Ten guards approached us, welcoming us and offering us bowls of beans and rice to restore our energy and water to replenish our flasks. They knew the guide and traded a few words with her, asked whether we'd encountered any creatures. No one ever did on the crossings, yet the forest retained its reputation as a place of mortal danger.

The guards fanned out, each approaching one of us in the group of crossers, smiling, asking how we'd found the journey, making pleasant inquiries about our island. The document checks were cursory, and I'd have passed undetected had it not been for the most extraordinary bad luck.

As my guard approached me, and I saw his face in the moonlight, I thought he looked familiar. Perhaps someone from my sister's living block? Someone I'd seen on my previous visit? Bad luck, for sure, but I doubted he'd remember me. Then I realized, and my stomach fell away. He was my neighbor's brother. He was a little younger, for sure, but their faces were unmistakably the same. In a rush, I remembered conversations I'd overheard between him and my neighbor on the communal telephone in the living block we shared on my island; and I remembered my neighbor afterward telling me his brother had a new job. Now I stood there in front of him, holding papers filled out in his brother's name, carrying his brother's identity card, trying to steal the single crossing his brother would be permitted that year.

The next few seconds were excruciating as I waited for realization to dawn. At first, confusion furrowed his brow as he read my permit, followed by understanding, which smoothed it again. He stepped forward and knocked me to the ground.

* * *

Eighteen hours later, I was standing at a different gate, waiting to make another crossing, this time to the smallest of the three correctional islands. After I'd been pulled roughly to my feet by two other guards from where my neighbor's brother had floored me, I'd been detained in a small shed next to the entrance gate. It was stacked with shovels and buckets, tarpaulins and wooden boards, presumably stored here in anticipation of the flood season, when the ground on the islands would turn to soup.

At one point, a guard I didn't recognize opened the door to ask me whether my neighbor knew that I was crossing in his name. I said he didn't. I explained that I'd stolen the identity card. She slammed the door shut without another word.

It transpired later that they'd got a judge on the telephone and were conducting a cursory trial among themselves. Since I was admitting all wrongdoing, they didn't seem to think anything more was required, and the judge agreed. After another few hours passed, I was told the verdict. I would cross to Correctional Island C3, where I'd be given Form 7α. That would present me with my options.

When the time came to cross, I was unaccompanied, as all prisoners are. You commit your crime alone, and you face your punishment alone, and no guard's life will be risked crossing between islands with you. Besides, there was nowhere to run. The narrow path I followed that night was walled in on either side by great vines covered with a hundred types of moss and vast fallen palms that stretched out across the forest's floor like mile-high pins knocked down in a bowling alley. The forest was impenetrable.

I made the crossing in three hours. As I reached the gate to the correctional island, my water canteen was empty, and my feet ached. My welcome was polite, gentle, almost kind, but a little weary and impersonal, as if the lines were learned by rote, which I'm sure they were. The custodians on these islands are proud to take their titles literally. They are there not to inflict your punishment on you but to assist you in undertaking it yourself. Just as a forest guide helps you cross, a custodian helps you atone. But unlike the guides, they don't endure the experience with you.

* * *

After refilling my canteen, the gentle man who had welcomed me took me to a small room in a long, low building by the gate and handed me Form 7α, a little red ink pad, and a rubber stamp. The options in the list were presented using cryptic euphemisms, but we all knew what they meant. We all learned our civic history at knowledge gatherings in our childhood, and as adults, we passed it on to the next generation in the same way.

* * *

Option 1. Induced sleep. Duration: two seasons.

During the year for which this punishment lasts, your consciousness is simply switched off. You lie on a bed in the island's infirmary, and two cannulas are placed in the veins that run up the inside of your forearms. Through one, flow the chemicals that, for two full seasons, keep you in a dreamless sleep; through the other, flow the nutrients and fluids that keep you alive. Custodians move you gently each day to avoid bed sores, and occasionally they stand you upright as a prophylactic against some unspecified condition you might develop. You're unaware of it all.

The grand theory of our new correctional techniques was devised fifty years ago when the islands were first inhabited. It states our collective intention that this option should be painless. The punishment it offers entails no suffering. You simply lose a year of your conscious life. In reality, those who had experienced it said the physical rehabilitation you need after you leave the infirmary is torture, your withered muscles trying to regain their strength, your body adjusting to being vertical again.

In any case, the option was scored through on my form: unavailable. In theory, they score through the option they think the prisoner will prefer. Like so many features of our lives, this was a compromise with the hardliners among the original settlers, who had felt it made a mockery of the purpose of punishment to allow the prisoner any say at all in its nature. In reality, however, I suspect they removed this option for me simply because they didn't want me out of the workforce for a whole year and then useless and weak for a further season as my body recovered.

* * *

Option 2. Elevated productivity. Duration: one season.

In every society that attempts to eschew hierarchy and privilege and live together as equals, there arises the question of those tasks so repellent that no one wants to do them. For our islands, as for so many such communities, they are the processing of sewage and the disposal of the dead. Were it not for our ecological austerity, we might dispose of both in the forest, the first to nourish the plants and beetles, the second to feed the carrion birds and the carnivores. But that is not our ethos. We neither add anything to the forest nor extract anything from it.

In the early days, some suggested that this detested work should be done by everyone, perhaps allocated on a schedule, so that for five days in each season, this would be your job. Others thought there would be sufficient volunteers provided certain extra privileges were offered as an inducement: an extra crossing per year, perhaps, or a stipend on top of your salary. But the policy that prevailed was that prisoners would do it. So it was added to Form 7α as an option. And for me, it remained available.

* * *

Option 3. Extended solitude. Duration: half season.

My mother had told us that, in the old world, prisoners would call this "the box" or "the hole," and custodians would call it "secure housing," and it might last tens of years. By any name, and for whatever duration, for us it means complete isolation in a small windowless one-roomed hut that is raised on stilts above the ground. The room contains an electric light, a mattress, a toilet, and a hatch. The walls are a dull white of the sort that looks dirty even when it's freshly painted. From the hatch, you retrieve the meals that the custodians bring you; a small green light above it indicates when one is available. The room is soundproofed so that you can neither talk with the custodians through the hatch nor hear the sounds of the forest around you. Nor, indeed, can the custodians hear any sounds you are moved to make in your solitude. As a result, when they open the door of a hut at the end of a sentence, they don't know what they might find. This option, too, was available to me.

* * *

Option 4. Enhanced displeasure. Duration: one week.

The shortest punishment, this was also the most feared. From what I've heard, it is always made available on Form 7α but almost never chosen. Like the box, it is undertaken in a small room in a soundproofed hut. Every morning at dawn for seven mornings in a row, a custodian arrives and injects your upper arm with a clear liquid. After five minutes, the pain floods in, consumes your whole body, and stays at a constant, quivering fever pitch until dusk, when the custodian returns with a second injection that relieves it. Then you go to bed and await the following day. For me, as for everyone, this was available.

* * *

Option 5. Reduced privilege. Duration: in perpetuity.

This was available to me as it usually is to anyone young and reasonably healthy. For those nearer to death, it is not considered a sufficient punishment, though from the beginning, some had asked what we thought we were achieving by punishing them anyway. I could choose this option and walk straight off the correctional island and return home. My identity card would be marked with a small orange dot in the upper right-hand corner. Nothing more. I'd only start to feel the effects gradually. When I applied to make a crossing, and my application was denied with no reason given; when some undesirable task would become necessary on my island, and I'd find myself added to the list of the volunteers without volunteering; when I saw my name at the bottom of the list for the communal telephone every time I asked to use it, and never on the list at all when any excess food became available. A lifetime of small, unpredictable degradations and frustrations.

That option completed the list. The first was scored through, and I must choose from the remaining four. If I didn't, if I refused to make the choice, the custodians would choose on my behalf at random, and the duration of the selected punishment would triple. I picked up the little stamp, pressed it into the ink pad, and marked the third option: Option 3: Extended solitude. Duration: half season. "REQUESTED."

* * *

My first day in the box was the first time I really reflected on my situation. From the moment my neighbor's brother had discovered my crime, through the detention in the hut, the crossing, and then my arrival on the correctional island, I'd been in a haze, my mind deferring all thought until a later, more stable time. But inside the box, after the door closed and the custodian left, there was nothing further to wait for except my release in three months' time.

The absence of all sounds except the ones you make

yourself is unsettling at first, but it wasn't entirely unfamiliar to me. Sometimes, as a child, if I was awake and my sister wasn't snoring, if the rest of the living block was asleep and the forest had fallen silent, I'd enjoy the noiseless tranquility and wish it would last longer.

I thought of my sister now. I hadn't told her I'd be coming to visit, so she wouldn't be expecting me, but she'd surely expect my phone call in the evening, and she'd worry when it didn't come the first night, then the second, and then on and on. News of punishments spread quickly on the islands, but she'd become completely cut off from her living block, so it would take some time to reach her.

I thought of her worries about me pushing her deeper into her darkness, and it caused me a dull, deadening pain. She was condemned to her own solitude now. No one would read her stories in the evenings; no one would try to coax her out of the dark corners where her mind led her; no one was there to tug on that line that reached down into the deep black waters where she was currently suspended, easing her inch by inch back toward the surface.

That thudding, throbbing pain never left me my whole time inside that box. It became a constant companion, there when I switched off the light and slept, and there again when I woke. It was there in every dream I had.

I had imagined the chief horror that solitude would hold would be the absence of any stimulus from outside. And that surely is a horror, and it surely caused me great anguish. But solitude also robs you of agency, and I hadn't accounted for that. Just as the outside world cannot impinge on you, you can do nothing to change the outside world. I couldn't call my sister, couldn't write to her; I couldn't send word that I was well, or at least alive, couldn't tell her I'd be reading stories to her again on the telephone before long. And without that feeling that I was doing something to improve things for her, the pain I felt because of the pain I knew she felt stayed, stubbornly unchanging, the same shape sitting in my gut from the start until near the end when it morphed into something far worse.

But, before that, there was something else to face, for I quickly realized that the mind is held together more by external forces than by inner strength. And what the box most surely removes are external forces.

For so long, I'd harbored this illicit dream of running off into the forest to find solitude. Away from the noise of the living block, away from the tedium of my work shifts, away from the neighbors and friends who want to bend my ear to complain about their partners or gossip about their relatives. Away from the constant little taps, prods, and nudges that the social world inflicts every day. And yet, there inside that box for half a season with the green light that signaled mealtimes as the only intrusion from the outside world, I realized how much I needed those taps and prods and nudges. My mind, waking from sleep each day, set off ideas running like a pack of mice released from a sack. Off they'd scurry, and soon some would be approaching perilous areas. Outside the box, I'd get distracted before any idea could go too far out of bounds. The distraction would slow it down, maybe remove it altogether, or set it on a better course. It would do the same with the good thoughts, too, of course, slow them down, remove them sometimes, and that's what made me long for solitude, somewhere to let the good thoughts run their full distance. But in the box, with no distractions—nothing to impinge on my consciousness—it wasn't the good thoughts that were freed to follow their course but the bad ones, which reached deeper and deeper into the dangerous areas of my mind.

In the old world, my mother had told us, the box was not soundproofed, and prisoners held there would hear the custodians talk, and they'd hear the other inmates gibber and scream as their minds unraveled, and they'd pray it wouldn't happen to them. When the penal code for our islands was written, it was thought more humane to soundproof the huts. But what looks less barbaric to those who've never experienced it very often isn't. Within two weeks, I was screaming at the walls that I wanted to change my choice on Form 7α. I wanted the needle and the pain it brought. Surely no thought was possible in the midst of that agony. Surely that would stop me from thinking.

* * *

By the end of the first month, I became seriously concerned about the state of mind in which I'd leave the box. I'd once heard stories of a man who couldn't be alone after his time inside. Even the hubbub and jostling of the living blocks weren't enough for him. He needed to always talk. He wore down friend after friend and lover after lover with his insatiable need for contact. He became a beggar, not for money because we had none of that, but for company.

I'd also met a woman who'd started to hallucinate in here and couldn't stop after she'd been released. Her mind had created companions for her. At first, she could hear them only, their voices seeming to come from the walls; but gradually, they assumed bodies, dressed in clothes, and sat beside her to talk.

She described their clothes to me one day as long tunics with elaborate embroidery. As she talked, her eyes stared past me at something a little way off. When I turned to look, it was an empty space.

I couldn't let this happen to me, so I tried to devise a strict regimen to keep my mind intact. I had no pencil or paper, so I couldn't write them down, but perhaps I could make up stories and tell them to myself as if I were telling them to my sister. Then I'd have something to share with her when we saw each other again. But the stories soon became overwrought, tangled, a profusion of detail and spandrels and tangents, obsessively pursued. As before, my mind simply could not supply on its own the boundaries, the myriad pushbacks, and corrections that any listener besides me might have provided. The mice, unconstrained, just ran where they would.

My next plan was to slow my thought processes. On Form 7α, the option that offers induced sleep lasts four times as long as the option that offers the box, an acknowledgment that having no consciousness at all, being as it were in a temporary death, is to be preferred to being conscious in this soundless solitude. So I aimed to bring my mind as close to sustained unconsciousness as it would let me.

I found I couldn't force myself to sleep for most of the day, and as I tried to sleep longer and longer, my dreams became more and more like the tangled, tortured stories I'd been telling myself before.

My mother had told us once of something her parents used to do in the old world. They'd sit, a group of strangers in a circle, and just breathe. As thoughts would arrive in their mind, they'd simply observe them, dismiss them, and return their attention to their breath. So I tried that. After a few days, it began to work, and I enjoyed some respite from my thoughts. But now the pendulum swung to its other extreme, which was boredom. At first, I welcomed it. To be bored after a month of frenetic, unloosed thoughts was bliss. I felt my whole body melt into the blankness of my mind, and I'd lose myself for hours on end. But true boredom, sustained over time, is not how you imagine. You think it will be an absence. But in reality, it becomes a real, substantial thing, like a thick tarry liquid that builds in your stomach and rises through your chest cavity and stands in your throat, ready to choke you.

* * *

The mind will only tolerate so much stasis, or at least mine will. As I entered my final month in the box, the mania of the thoughts returned, and all my attempts to dismiss them did not work. It was at this time that the pain I felt because of my sister's suffering grew, changed shape, and threatened to undo me. Through the final month, my mind was clenched not just by pain but also by guilt.

The thought haunted me that I had done this to her. Because of me, she had spent two months already in complete solitude, cut off from me and from her living block, and another month lay ahead. I was to blame for that. That gave a twist to the pain that was already there and had been there constantly throughout the past two months. It brought it fully to life, made it hum in my abdomen as if there was an electric current running through it. Pain, with a buzzing electric corona of guilt. I had been rash. I'd made a half-baked plan that was unlikely to succeed, and I'd got myself caught. *But you did it for me*, I heard my sister say in my head, and in the perfect silence of the room, the words sounded loud enough to be real, and I thought of the woman who could not shake her hallucinations. But I wondered whether my sister was right about this. Had I truly done it selflessly? Or was I not simply trying to recover something— her—that was so crucial to my own happiness?

But still, there was more to feed my guilt. More and worse. After all, I had chosen this option, three months of solitude. I could have chosen a week of chemical pain instead. That was available to me on my Form 7α. If I'd chosen that, I would have been free seven weeks ago. I would have been able to call her every evening for the past seven weeks. Instead, I would be leaving my sister an extra eleven weeks alone, and I did it because I was too frightened of their needle and the pain it would deliver.

You think your love is unconditional. Form 7α disabused me of that.

It was this, among everything else that happened in there, that came closest to breaking me. I couldn't dislodge the thought. I was the author of all this. No one but me bore any responsibility for it. I had sent my sister into the deepest solitude at exactly the time when she was least able to bear it. Like a Catherine wheel firework, the guilt spun in my mind, its sparks touching every corner, singeing wherever they landed.

Form 7α was to be a centerpiece of our new egalitarian society. When you err, there is no authority above you who chooses your punishment, no executioner who metes it out. The choice is yours, and the custodians are there only to assist— stagehands who set the scene and pass you the props. As the final days of my time in the box dragged on, and I found myself crouching in the corner of the hut, clenching my hair in my fists, the deep anguish of my guilt always on the cusp of overwhelming me, I wondered whether those who had created that form had ever imagined what it would do.

* * *

No one talks much of the custodians who staff these correctional islands. As with the job of judge and gate guard, this is not a vocation for which you can apply in our society. Rather, you are approached if the relevant committee thinks you might be suitable. If they deem you kind, resilient, fair, in general, virtuous, then they will ask you to consider this post. The joke goes that if you don't want the job, it's yours. But this presents a paradox. Those invited to become custodians are those least likely to agree, and we never compel anyone to do work they do not wish to do. Unless they're prisoners, of course. So they are enticed partly with longer periods of leave and earlier dates for retirement but also with a reverence paid communally by all the people of our society. While we do not talk of them often, the custodians know that they are esteemed. The committee has deemed them virtuous people, and we together respect that judgment. It's surprising, or surprising to me, the power of our fellows' esteem in a society like ours.

When my custodian opened the door of my hut to release me on the final day of my sentence, what I noticed first were the sounds. A flock of blue macaws swept overhead and turned as one rippling entity, banking west, and the swish of their feathers and the scream of their calls filled my ears, the first sound not of my own making that I'd heard for three months. They disappeared toward the setting sun, which was beginning to fill the sky with its colors, as if orange and purple ink was seeping into blue blotting paper, creeping across it. As their calls receded, I heard the gentle background buzz of the insects that live near the forest's edge and the light flutter of the leaves in the trees brushing against one another.

What I noticed second, after the sounds and the sky, was the custodian's face. It betrayed a sort of wariness, and his body looked tensed in anticipation of trouble. He would have none from me, and I smiled quickly and thanked him to signal that I bore him no ill will. It stayed with me, though, the learned caution that his look betrayed. I wondered what he had seen before when he'd opened that door.

Two hours after my release, I was taken to the gate on the other side of the correctional island from the one where I'd entered. My canteen was filled with fresh water, and my custodian set me on my way back to my home island with a tired smile and a hackneyed joke about hoping never to see me again while he was at work. I smiled in return, strapped on the red headlamp he gave me, and began my journey. Island C3, where I spent my solitude, lies halfway between my sister's island and my own, and I arrived at the gates to mine in a little under four hours. While I'd tried to keep active in the box, there is a limit to what's possible. So, as I trekked through the thick oozing mud and tripped on the hidden ferns that crisscrossed the forest path, my legs were weak, and I had to stop a number of times and rest on a vine branch to catch my breath.

As I reentered my island through the gate I had left illegally three months before, I felt that strange dislocation that occurs when you find a place familiar but know the person through whose eyes you saw it before is not the person you've become who sees it now. I made my way across the island to my living block as the sun started to rise. As I got closer and closer to my neighborhood, I knew more and more of the people I passed. They were leaving for work as I was returning home, and they greeted me warmly. I would go to work again tomorrow morning, but today I was given to acclimatize.

We pride ourselves here on treating Form 7α as the last word on a person's punishment. Once you have undertaken whatever sentence you choose from it, your crime is of no further consequence. Your debt is paid, and you return to society to be treated exactly as you were before. We have agreed, collectively, that these punishments are sufficient and no further sanction is required; we believe, collectively, that a crime teaches us nothing of the perpetrator's character and everything about the contingencies that might land any one of us in their position. Individually, of course, many of us dissent from this opinion.

So, as I entered my living block, I was greeted by my neighbors as if I had hardly left. As I approached the door to my living space, I noticed it was ajar, and a pair of sandals sat neatly arranged outside. I assumed it was a friend who'd come by to open my rooms and let out the stagnant air that must have built up while they lay empty. But when I pushed the door open, I saw instead my sister sitting in the wicker chair by the window, her head resting on a cushion, her eyes closed, and her hands holding one another loosely in her lap. As I gently shut the door, she awoke, and I could see immediately that the shadow had lifted from her mind, and her eyes once again held that special light that shone through so many of my childhood memories. Her face, soft and blank in sleep, broke into a grin as she woke up, half mischievous, half apprehensive, looking at me and knowing that we had both endured so much since we were last able to laugh together and wondering whether it had robbed us of the chance to do so again.

* * *

Even now, from the far vantage point of the future, I find it hard to describe the next three days we spent together. I can say how we spent our time, of course. On the first day, my sister cooked for us the meal my mother had always made on our birthdays. "As close to decent, old-world food as you can get out here," she used to say, and my sister mimicked her voice as she served it up for us in my rooms, and we both laughed. That night we talked about our mother until the sun set, and we went to sleep. My sister walked with me to work in the morning and met me there again at the end of my shift, and we walked along the fence that separated the island from the forest and watched a flock of macaws overhead and an army of ants underfoot. Then I cooked for her, and we fell asleep as the sun set again. The third day was the same, except that my neighbors dropped in as we were finishing dinner. Some had met my sister on previous visits; others, I think, were just curious because they knew I'd gone to the box for trying to visit her.

So, yes, I can tell the events of these days well enough. But the emotions that ran through them are much less clear to me.

On the first night, about halfway from sunset to sunrise, I was shaken out of sleep by a nightmare in which I was stranded alone in the forest. I turned over and looked up to see my sister at the window crying, the tears on her cheek catching the moonlight. I said nothing, and in time she lay down again. I think we both remained awake until the sun rose, and it was time for me to leave for work. By then, she was smiling and joking and asking what we should make for dinner.

As the sun set on her final day, she prepared her backpack for the crossing back to her home island. We walked over to the gate together. The same guards were on duty who had unwittingly let me pass illegally that night three months ago. One of them stiffened when they saw me, but the others paid me no attention. My sister and I embraced, and she said to me, low and choked, her voice cracking, "I'm so sorry you ever had to make that choice." I didn't reply. I couldn't begin to think how I should. She turned and left through the gate.

* * *

For the next decade, we visited one another each year for however long our work would grant us leave. We adhered to the law, each of us crossing just once every two seasons. My sister's depression fell into a long remission, and I began to wonder whether she was free of it completely. But in the ninth year, it returned, and I started to think instead that it would never leave again.

History repeated itself with small changes. I made one crossing at the beginning of the year, just as the flood season gave way to the dry. I found my sister in a desperate state. I crossed back but knew I couldn't remain another two seasons without seeing her again. As the evening phone calls became harder and harder to bear, I knew the time was approaching when I would have to try again.

I made it further this time than last. I made the crossing, I was waved through by the guards on my sister's island, and I even managed to spend the last two days with her before they found me. It seems a neighbor reported yesterday that I was missing from my living block. They haven't told me who it was, and I guess they never will, but I suspect I know.

* * *

So here I sit again with Form 7α, the little rubber stamp, and the pad of red ink. At this moment ten years ago, I made a choice that taught me something I never wanted to know. This time, I won't let it teach me anything at all.

My custodian returns to the room and asks for the form, and I hand it back. She looks at it and sees I've left it blank. She looks at me and frowns a little. She starts to return it to me. She opens her mouth to explain how the system works, that if I don't make a choice, she'll choose at random, and the duration will triple. I shake my head and raise my palm to stop her, for I know all that. After a moment, she nods and leaves the room. I exhale and sit back to wait while she determines my sentence.

* * *

This story first appeared in the After Dinner Conversation—October 2023 issue.

Discussion Questions

1. If you were forced to fill out the punishment form, which punishment would you choose and why?
2. Do you think the various punishment options are roughly equal, or are certain ones worse/better? What makes them so?
3. Why did the narrator leave his punishment form blank at the end of the story?
4. Are certain rational and reasonable crimes, like illegally traveling to visit a suffering family member, moral? Or are laws meant to impose a collective benefit but an individual loss? Was the narrator right to break the law?
5. The society in the story believes "a crime teaches us nothing of the perpetrator's character and everything about the contingencies that might land any one of us in their position." What does this mean, and do you agree or disagree?

* * *

Conscience Cleaners

Alexander B. Joy

* * *

[W]e are free from the unsupportable burden of an accusing, tormenting conscience,—a misery that none can bear: and therefore let us praise Him for His preventing grace, and say, Every misery that I miss is a new mercy.

Izaak Walton, *The Compleat Angler* (Part I, Chapter XXI)

* * *

Esteemed members of the Grand Rectification Council, my intention today is not to revisit what my client Mr. Henmore has done. His prior actions, however heinous, belong to an irretrievable and unalterable past. It is not our place to fixate on what cannot be changed—to remain in thrall to events that have hardened beyond our powers of correction. If our objective is justice, our focus must be the present, and what can be accomplished in this still malleable instant to ensure that the days to come will promote less cruelty than those we leave behind.

To this end, I am about to ask you to accept a proposition that at first may seem too radical even to countenance. But I trust that, if you consider the particulars of this case, you will agree that my request is consistent with the Council's ongoing pursuit of a fair and just world. Further, I am hopeful that you will be moved to grant what I request without delay. I stress that this is no mere stunt in service of legal legerdemain. The Devil has enough advocates. I am here to appeal to your better angels.

The facts in the matter before us, none of which are in dispute, are these. Decades ago, Mr. Henmore committed a crime affronting the laws of state and human decency alike. He was tried for this trespass in accordance with our typical protocols and procedures. In light of the available evidence, Mr. Henmore was found guilty of the charges brought against him, prompting the court to issue a sentence slightly less severe than the allowable maximum. And, as of last year, Mr. Henmore has served enough of that sentence for the state to declare his debt to society discharged. He was released early, and as we speak he walks the streets a free man.

Yet, although Mr. Henmore has served his time, his punishment has not ceased.

What do I mean by this? Here I refer you to Exhibit A, the report filed in the wake of Mr. Henmore's most recent psychiatric evaluation. (You may notice that it is the latest entry in a long series. Let the record reflect that Mr. Henmore began undertaking these visits on a voluntary basis several months after his release.) The report's author, our respected colleague Dr. Lathkin, notes in Mr. Henmore a profusion of symptoms more commonly observed in the profoundly religious and those enduring post-traumatic stress—in other words, symptoms indicative of a serious mental health condition. Dr. Lathkin tells us that Mr. Henmore suffers daily (according to her notes, almost hourly) from intrusive, uncontrollable thoughts that, in addition to bringing him emotional anguish, induce debilitating physical reactions that impair his everyday functioning. By Dr. Lathkin's account, Mr. Henmore faces surges of depression and anxiety, sudden panic attacks involving cold sweats and respiratory difficulties, recurrent bouts of extreme nausea, physical aches in the heart and head and abdomen, and intense dissociative episodes that leave him disoriented and terrified. Each sounds unpleasant on its own, but in conjunction, they form an unendurable syndrome.

Lest the Council suspect Dr. Lathkin or myself of hyperbole, let me draw your attention to Exhibit B, a video recording of Mr. Henmore at home. While your neurolink loads the file, allow me to highlight two crucial details regarding the footage you are about to watch. First, in this video, Mr. Henmore is not playacting in any way. At the time of the recording, he had no idea the camera was even there; the entire clip was collected without his knowing via a miniature lens hidden in the screw-hole of an electrical outlet. Which brings us to the second important detail. Rest assured that this video was collected legally, thanks to the surveillance powers established under the SCUM Act of 2065, which entitles law enforcement to monitor certain types of offenders in perpetuity. Ah, there! Finally loaded. Let's proceed.

The figure seated on the sofa is Mr. Henmore. We catch him during a slow, rainy weekend—notice the trails of water beading on the windows—where the forecast promises the bland entertainments of gray days spent indoors. Mr. Henmore has responded accordingly. You see that he sits alone; that the television is turned off, and no other screens loom anywhere in sight; that he is not hooked up to a neurolink terminal (and that his home ostensibly lacks the infrastructure for it); that his lone source of stimulation in this moment is the newspaper blanketing his lap. I'm sure you will agree that nothing about the scene appears moving enough to precipitate what follows. And yet.

Watch as, without provocation, the paper bunches in his clenching fists. He looks up and away, at some neutral point on the wall. He knows what's about to happen, and is doing his best to steel himself for it. Even at this distance, you can tell his breaths are coming short and frantic—the body desperate for air in a room where there is suddenly not enough. He begins to wheeze. I will remain quiet for a moment so that you can hear him gasp like a beached fish. Now his heart, tricked by some bestial memory into thinking it must enable the body to flee or fight, thunders and palpitates at random intervals. (Notice him clutch his chest. I'm told that panic attacks of lesser severity than this feel like impending cardiac arrest. How, in so trying a moment, is the afflicted to tell the difference?) His brow gleams, slick with sweat. Now he's on the floor, curled in the defensive posture of a body threatened on all sides. And look—from this angle, the camera's lens points directly into his eyes. Note the dilation of his pupils; the human eye grows greedy for light when threatened, the better to perceive nearby dangers.

When you finish observing him from a clinical perspective, I urge you to focus on those eyes, and consider what you see in them.

What you have witnessed here is a small sample of the

agonies Mr. Henmore experiences multiple times each day, every day. What's more, Dr. Lathkin confirms in her analyses that Mr. Henmore's overwhelming symptoms have persisted for years, developing during his incarceration, and stalking him unto the present. The good doctor has not left Mr. Henmore to fend for himself, of course. She has tried an array of established and emerging therapies, but regrets to inform us that all such regimens have proven ineffective. The prognosis is clear: Mr. Henmore will not recover from his condition, and it is uncertain how much longer he will last under its crushing burden. Not unless we take drastic action to excise its root cause.

But what, then, causes Mr. Henmore's suffering? I have a pair of documents for us to consult that will help us answer that question—and point us toward the solution.

Let's start with Exhibit C, the findings of the parole board that gave Mr. Henmore his freedom. A cursory review shows that they based their decision on three elements. The first—and admittedly most essential from a parole board's perspective—was their sincere belief that Mr. Henmore posed no further danger to society. Why did they believe this? Because of the other two elements they cited. The parole board acknowledged Mr. Henmore's many years of good behavior as a contributing factor in their decision. They also deemed Mr. Henmore a man fully and truly repented of his past transgressions. In their view, his contrition was genuine. But one line in particular from their verdict merits further scrutiny. "The Henmore we release today," they affirm, "is a completely different man than the Henmore who was sent to prison." Consider the analysis of character implicit in this statement. The board's conclusion here is less that Mr. Henmore has made good on his crimes than that he has become constitutionally incapable of repeating them.

Indeed, we should feel no compunctions against labeling Mr. Henmore a man transformed. The former Mr. Henmore, as his criminal actions attest, had been a creature deficient of conscience. But he recedes ever further into the past, supplanted by the Mr. Henmore of today, whose conscience now performs with arguably greater acuteness than yours or mine. And this leads us to the root of Mr. Henmore's suffering. To elaborate, I present my other document: Exhibit D, a compilation of psychometric tests from the reputable and licensed professionals that Dr. Lathkin solicited for second opinions regarding Mr. Henmore's case. The methods of Drs. Derwent, Swarkeston, and Humber vary according to their specialties (and also by how invasive their penetrations into Mr. Henmore's skull and gray matter), but ultimately their reports differ only in their phrasing. Independently of one another, all three reach the same conclusions. Namely:

1) Mr. Henmore's remorse is neither faked nor self-serving, but entirely genuine.

2) Mr. Henmore is a substantively changed man, whose metamorphoses of character, conscience, and constitution mean that he could never again perform the ghastly acts he has done in the past.

3) Mr. Henmore's extreme emotional and physical reactions are products of his remorse, triggered by the inescapable memories of his past deeds.

The portrait of the harsh dynamics at work in my client's case at last coheres. Mr. Henmore is a new man, equipped with both the moral understanding necessary for living with decency, and a fundamentally changed character that prohibits his being anything but decent. Yet, precisely because he has become a decent person, the tangle of memory and conscience weaves destructive consequences. I trust that the situation's bitter irony is not lost on the Council. Mr. Henmore's lengthy time behind bars has reformed him as intended—but due to that reformation, he now experiences unimaginable suffering as his conscience slowly kills him.

The cruelty of this arrangement—dare we call it an especially virulent strain of *damnatio memoriae?*—far exceeds what even our most stringent penalties prescribe. Yet it is within your powers to redress.

The Council will recall that the Armed Forces' considerable strides in neural correction number among the many innovations to emerge from the first of the Potable Water Wars. Initially, neural correction induced a sweeping amnesia of whole segments of the patient's life, which at the time was sufficient for the military's stated therapeutic purposes. (That it purged our returning veterans' entire recollection of the conflict was simply an added bonus.) In the intervening years, this technology has evolved to a point where individual memories can be erased with targeted precision, much in the same way that a surgeon excises only a body's diseased tissue while leaving its healthy parts intact. Typically, neural correction is reserved for military applications alone, but is permitted for other uses where our courts approve them. Therefore, following the recommendations of Dr. Lathkin and her peers as outlined here in Exhibit E, I request that the Council approve this treatment for my client.

At bottom, it is a straightforward proposition. The guilt of a truly repented person causes him real suffering and tangible

AFTER DINNER CONVERSATION

harm. He is no longer the kind of person who requires the unceasing reminder of that painful memory in order to prevent him from doing wrong in the future. Therefore, in consideration of the fact that this memory of his serves no purpose other than inflicting harm upon him—adding still more pain to a world that possesses a surfeit thereof—I contend that its removal is the only just course.

I understand that the Council might hesitate to grant this petition, if not object outright. Why allow a man to forget the enormity of his past sins? Perhaps it sounds too much like a privilege, rather than a mercy—and society has often been reluctant to confer privileges upon those like Mr. Henmore, who have not always walked a righteous path.

But to let ourselves remain beholden to the attitudes and values of an unenlightened past is no way to administer justice. Objections of this nature all implicitly insist that certain kinds of people ought to suffer. Under such an outlook, justice cannot be restorative, only retributive. Its goal is never redemption for one who has strayed from the moral course, but for that person to face torment in perpetuity, with neither the ability nor the opportunity to seek repentance. Yet this approach is a recipe for a world containing more punishment than crime, whose sole response to pain is to generate more of it. So punitive a system, O Council, is too monstrous a prospect for us to tolerate.

Still, one question remains for us to resolve. What of the victim? All crimes have their wronged parties. Is it fair to the victim in this case if we rid Mr. Henmore of the memory of what he has done? At risk of sounding callous, I humbly suggest that the opinion of the victim is irrelevant to the matter at hand.

The state has traditionally—or as a matter of practicalit—

assumed that the swift application of justice is the appropriate salve for whatever injury a victim has sustained. After all, if we were to entrust victims to dispense their own verdicts and sentences, there would be no guarantee of their acting in a manner promoting the general welfare. We risk them taking their vengeance without regard for precedent, inviting the global blindness that is the endgame of trading an eye for an eye. (There is also the logistical matter of seeking redress for a party that no longer numbers among the living, in which case, the pursuit of restitution must necessarily fall to the state.) But here we must not conflate justice with forgiveness. The power to forgive lies only with the wronged party. If one man harms a second, it would be absurd for a third to step in and forgive the first when this third man has sustained no wrong. In all matters brought before the courts, the state occupies the position of this third man. Yet the state—the apparatus we have been commanded to pilot—has never assumed the power to forgive, nor the responsibility to compel forgiveness. It has chosen as its duty the fostering of peace and safety, intervening only when it has determined that an act poses serious risk to them. To this end, justice concerns itself not with matters of the heart, but of the soul—not with the gratification of individual passions and rages, but with maintaining a safe and secure haven that allows all under its aegis the opportunity to discover and become their best selves.

Even so, these questions of procedure and intent have little bearing on our present concerns. In Mr. Henmore's case, we must accept that the matter is moot. No dissent is forthcoming from the wronged party. She cannot be reached for comment. And whereof we cannot speak, thereof we must be silent.

The reality remains unchanged despite these supposed complications. What we must contend with is this: Under our watch, the guilt of a truly repented person causes them real suffering, deserved only according to the most barbaric metric of justice. We must ask ourselves whether that person deserves to be saddled with such an agonizing corrective mechanism now that the need for it has long since passed. And we must ensure that we are prepared to live with the answer.

Worthy members of the Grand Rectification Council, the decision to end Mr. Henmore's torture lies with you, and you alone.

We await your wise judgment.

* * *

This story first appeared in the After Dinner Conversation—September 2021 issue.

Discussion Questions

1. If you were on the Council, would you vote to remove Mr. Henmore's memory of the crime he did and relieve him of the pain of his guilt? Should a person be forced to live with the lifetime guilt of their past actions?

2. Would your opinion be different if Mr. Henmore was suffering not from the guilt of what he did, but from the experience of being in prison? Would you support removing the memory of the trauma of having been in prison? What, if anything, is the difference between the two?

3. Do you think it is possible for someone to suffer for years, or a lifetime, for the remorse they feel for a wrong they have done? Should they take steps to seek help for that pain, or is that pain required? If so, for what purpose?

4. Would you permit Mr. Henmore to remove the memory if the mental trauma was not for a crime he committed, but for a non-criminal wrong he committed instead?

5. What is the purpose of prison and the judicial system? Is it to deter crime, to punish those who commit the crime, or something else? Which, if any, of these does Mr. Henmore's continued suffering serve?

* * *

Blackorwhite

Jay Allisan

* * *

He's on the shitter the first time I see him: pants around his ankles, shirttail hanging between his legs, eyes shut and mouth corkscrewed with effort. The guard admits me to the cell and locks it again once I'm inside. Before I can say a word, the prisoner hollers, "Hang on, fellas, here it comes!" and what follows is a rambunctious round of flatulence and defecation that makes me grimace. When it's over he cracks open one eye.

"They never let me have cheese," he says, "on account of what it does to my guts."

Another blast echoes inside the toilet. His face is red and strained but he's grinning now. I count five teeth, two of which are rotten.

"You must be Mr. Morley," I say.

"Ain't nobody calls me that. Call me Fuzzy. You must be the doc."

His left hand is shackled to the bar beside him. He sticks out the other. In light of where he's sitting, I decline the gesture.

He just shrugs and scratches his behind.

"Sorry to get you down here in the middle of the night," Fuzzy says. "I told 'em it's only the cheese. Doc Yardley knows all about it."

Fuzzy's head is as glassy as a contact lens. Shapeless tattoos adorn his arms. His chest is sunken but his belly is round. He's 71, though that seems like an underestimation. He shifts to the left as he passes gas, his toes curling.

"Yes, I've had a quick look at your file," I answer. "How long ago was your meal?"

"Couple hours. Still got a ways to go. I only been sittin' here for half that, give 'er take. Yep, still got a long ways to go. Doc Yardley knows all about it."

It's nearing midnight. I left my wife and infant daughter at home. The forecast calls for heavy rain, and our new property lies at the end of a dirt road. At this point, there's not much I can do. To be called out at all for lactose intolerance is profoundly irritating.

Best just to get this over with.

I lay my bag on the cot and find some quick-dissolve loperamide. I pop two pills from the foil and give them to Fuzzy.

"I expect it's too late for these. You'll just have to ride it out. Be sure to keep hydrated."

Fuzzy gives me his gummy grin.

"I appreciate that, doc. It's not so bad. Worth it, if you ask me."

He farts loudly. I return the medicine to my bag. Fuzzy says, "Boy, I love cheese. You like cheese, doc?"

I close my bag and indicate for the guard to open the door. "Sure."

"Didn't always do me like this, you know. I 'member goin' into a house once and there bein' a big block 'a cheese just sittin' there in the fridge, and without even meanin' to I just took a bite of it. Mo found me there munchin' away, and he said that the police had ways 'a findin' you based on your teeth prints. He said I hadda take it with me or else I would get caught, so I took it and I ate the whole thing. It was better'n winnin' the lottery.

"Course, that's why I never went to the dentist," Fuzzy says. "Didn't want them to get no teeth prints. Mo said if I'd just not eat stuff when we was doin' a job then it wouldn't be a problem, but I couldn't help it. All them 'lectronics meant nothin' to me. I just wanted to see what's in the fridge.

"He looked out for me, you know. I don't care what no one says, he were the best big brother a kid could ask for. Always let me tag along. He was the one who took me for ice cream on my birthday, and he was the one who gave me my bicycle. He said it were from him and Momma, but I knew it were really from him. He just didn't want Momma to feel bad. She'd cry sometimes, 'cuz she'd get sad she couldn't give us bicycles or new shoes, but Mo, he'd cheer her right up. He could do voices, you know, like characters. Momma always liked him to do Donald Duck. My favorite was Woody the Woodpecker. That laugh, boy, it cracked me up. That was Mo. Always good for a laugh. Hey doc, you mind gettin' me a drink? I got a cup there on the sink, but I don't wanna get up."

He grins toothlessly. I'm poised at the open door, but he's grinning at me, and it was my own recommendation.

"One moment," I say to the guard.

There's a stainless-steel cup on the stainless-steel sink atop the stainless-steel toilet tank, behind and above Fuzzy's head. I'm forced to stand beside the toilet while the cup fills. The smell is obnoxious.

"Thanks, doc. I sure appreciate it," he says when I hand him the cup, and once again I prepare to leave. Fuzzy's digestive tract rumbles thunderously, and what follows is the single longest fart I've ever heard, followed by what could be urination. Fuzzy presses a hand to his side, sweating.

"Ooh, boy. Next time they let me pick my meal, you remind me 'bout tonight, Ralph. Don't let me order no cheese."

"I think your problem was the cheesecake, Fuzzy," the guard answers. "Shouldn'tve eaten so much."

"What did they call it? White berry somethin'..."

"White chocolate raspberry," Ralph says. "White Chocolate Raspberry Explosion."

Fuzzy hoots. "You're kiddin'! Explosion? Boy, ain't that the truth! Real good, though. Haven't had cheesecake in years. You like cheesecake, doc?"

I remove my glasses and pinch the bridge of my nose. I should have left sooner, as soon as I gave him the loperamide. If I'd left then, I wouldn't have heard Fuzzy's latest outburst. I could have gone home with a clear conscience.

I set my medical bag back on the cot and unlatch it.

"I'll need a gallon jug filled with water," I tell Ralph. "And please bring salt and sugar."

The cell door clangs shut and Ralph departs. I search through my bag for a thermometer, which I place under Fuzzy's tongue. He talks out of the other side of his mouth.

"What's goin' on, doc? What's all this about? Doc Yardley ain't never bother with nothin' like this."

"It's only precautionary," I answer. "Nothing to worry

about. I need you to stand up."

"I don't think that's a good idea, doc. I'm just as like to shit if I'm standin'."

I pull on gloves. "It's only for a moment. Stand, please. Quickly."

He bunches his shirttail in his hand and rises on shaky legs. I see what I need to see in the toilet, then flush the putrid mess.

"Turn," I say, and Fuzzy presents me with his backside. He yelps when I prod him.

"Done," I say. "You can sit down now."

He sits, farting promptly. I remove my gloves and take back the thermometer. Fuzzy's watching me, his chest heaving.

"Is it bad, doc? Just give it to me straight, I can take it. Just give it to me straight."

"It's nothing to worry about. You're only dehydrated."

"Then what was with the finger up my—"

"Simply precautionary. There's nothing to worry about."

Ralph returns with the water, and packets of salt and sugar. I mix a rehydration solution and give the jug a shake. Behind me Fuzzy mutters to himself.

"Doc Yardley never stuck a finger up my ass. Why couldn't Doc Yardley—"

"My finger did not go up your ass," I say curtly. "You've been a prisoner for fifty-four years. I expect you would know the difference. As for Dr. Yardley, we both would have had a better evening had he not been unavailable, but as it is, we're stuck with one another. Drink this."

I hand him the jug. He pokes his tongue through the opening, licking the rim. He makes a face.

"Tastes like salt. I ain't gonna drink this."

"You have to."

"Well, I ain't gonna!"

I seat myself on the edge of the cot, lean forward, and narrow my eyes. "Then I'll be forced to give you an IV."

He looks at me blankly.

"It's a needle, Fuzz," says Ralph, and now he understands, and the flatulence begins in earnest as he writhes on his seat.

"No way, doc, I ain't gonna get no needle. You ain't comin' anywhere near me with no needle, no way no how, you just keep away from me or else I'm gonna... I'm gonna... ooh, boy..."

He slumps forward. I catch him before he can slide off the toilet, and push his head between his knees. I curse under my breath.

"How'd you know he hates needles?" Ralph asks. His expression is irritatingly amused.

"In his file. Though Dr. Yardley failed to mention the mere thought would make him faint." I curse again as Fuzzy starts to come round, catches a whiff of his own fumes, then retches all over his feet.

I should have left after I gave him the loperamide.

"Towels," I say to Ralph, kneading my brow. "A bucket. Disinfectant. And plenty of hot water."

Having thoroughly cleaned himself up, Fuzzy manages to remain upright as the cacophony inside the toilet continues. He sips the rehydration solution. Ralph convinced him it was better than the alternative.

"Still tastes like salt," he mutters, then belches. "Don't this come in other flavors?"

"No."

I need to see at least half the jug make it down Fuzzy's throat before I can, in good conscience, leave. He's hardly made a dent. The night is creeping on toward one o'clock.

Fuzzy takes a sip, making a face. "It's like drinkin' from the ocean. Mo always told me never to drink from the ocean. Why you makin' me do this, doc? This ain't no good for me."

"Just drink it," I say, rubbing my hand over my face. "I haven't got the energy to explain it to you."

He sends me a hurt look. "Mo always 'splained things to me, even if I didn't understand. He'd say it so I could. Taught me 'bout all sorts 'a things, like how to clean a fish, or fix the flat on a tire, or what to say when them men came 'round lookin' for Momma. I 'member he'd always check my spellin' homework before I'd go to bed. He must not 'a been much better at spellin' than me, cuz I never got better'n a C plus. But he checked it all the same. Always tryin' to help me out."

Fuzzy sips from his jug. "I don't s'pose you was ever a big brother, doc."

I give him a lean smile. "Fuzzy, would you like to hear about the transport of sodium through the phospholipid bilayers of the cell wall, and the osmotic flow of water from a solution of high concentration to one of low concentration?"

"You know, doc, you sound like Bad Jack when you say stuff like that. Like nobody knows anything 'cept for you. He was always makin' the rest of us feel stupid. Not even Mo knew what he was sayin' sometimes. Bad Jack, he read all kinds 'a books, books about history 'n art 'n stuff I never even heard of, like astral projection. I asked him about it once, and even though he talked at me all afternoon I still don't know what it is. All I know is the words. Ass-tral pro-jeck-shun. Mo said it's a bunch 'a hooey, but not to say that to Bad Jack. And he said if Bad Jack ever gave me some mushrooms, no matter what not to eat 'em.

"You had to watch out with Bad Jack sometimes. 'Course, back then we called him Black Jack, least till he made up his mind he didn't like that no more. Thought it was racist. I said to him, how can it be racist if you really are black, Jack, and he hit me so hard he knocked out three of my teeth. Right here."

Fuzzy points to an empty spot in his decidedly empty mouth. He makes a face as he passes gas, takes a sip from the jug, and makes a face again.

"Bad Jack was the idea man," Fuzzy says. "He's the one who'd say here's where we're gonna go, and here's what we're gonna take. The rest of us was just muscle. 'Cept for Mo. Bad Jack would talk with him sometimes, just the two of 'em. I figure Mo probably had some good ideas, too, but Bad Jack just said they were his.

"It was Mo's idea to make me lookout, I 'member that. I was too small at first to be much good for carryin' TVs, but Mo said to Bad Jack that I could spot the hairs on a toad from a hundred feet away, and I could whistle besides. If anyone was comin' I'd go like this."

Fuzzy fills his lungs, puckers his lips, and proceeds to spew saliva all over my face. Ralph hands me a fresh towel through the bars. Fuzzy gives an embarrassed grin.

"Sorry, doc. Guess my whistle's not what it used to be. Probably 'cuz I ain't got the right teeth."

"Just keep drinking," I mutter, and Fuzzy takes an obliging gulp. He gags, but he keeps it down.

"I was a good tree-climber, too," he says. "Could be up'n down lickety-split. We was in a pinch, once, 'cuz there was a neighbor across the street. He was walkin' back and forth in front 'a his window, watchin' the house, and I was up in the tree watchin' him, and when I saw him goin' for the phone I gave the whistle, zipped out of the tree, and was across the street faster'n you can say *meep-meep*."

He grins at me expectantly.

"That's the Roadrunner," he says, when I don't respond. His grin falters. "Mo could do it better."

I pinch the bridge of my nose with a sigh.

Fuzzy farts, looking dejected. His rehydration jug is still three-quarters full. From outside the cell Ralph says, "So what'd you do then, Fuzz? With the neighbor across the street."

For a moment I think he's not going to answer, but then he mumbles something under his breath.

Ralph puts a hand to his ear. "I can't hear you from over there. Say again?"

"I THREW A BRICK THROUGH HIS WINDOW!" Fuzzy bellows, and now he's grinning again, gleeful as a child. "Right through the front window, the best strike I ever threw. Got the whole plate!" He slaps his knee, hooting. "When he came runnin' to the door I shouted, 'Go back to where you came from, you damn Commie!' and then I ran away. I don't think he was a Commie," Fuzzy says, "but I just thought it was fun to say.

"That was the first time Bad Jack said somethin' nice to me. They got away clean, they did, with the TV and a stereo besides. All 'cuz of my diversion." He puffs his chest up proudly.

"Have a drink," I tell him, shaking my head. He takes a small swallow and burps.

"Bad Jack told me I did good. Said I was a real member of the gang now. The Domino Gang. Bad Jack said the name came from some Chinese army or somethin'. I thought it was 'cuz we was black and white.

"There was four of us: Bad Jack, Mo, me and Tyrone. Me and Mo was white, 'a course, and Bad Jack and Tyrone was black. Then there was Jamal, who did the fencin', and he—"

Fuzzy stops himself, looking at Ralph warily.

"I ain't gonna say nothin' about Jamal. He weren't in the gang proper. He weren't there the night it went bad."

"It's okay, Fuzz," Ralph says. "Nobody's asking you about Jamal."

"I reckon he's long gone anyhow. Might even be dead. He was older'n the rest of us, 'cept maybe for Bad Jack. It's hard to tell with black people, you know?"

Ralph, who's black, only grunts.

"But I ain't gonna say nothin' about him," Fuzzy says. "The Domino Gang ain't nothin' if not loyal. We stick together no matter what. Take care 'a each other."

"Have a drink," I say to Fuzzy. My watch is ticking steadily toward two.

Fuzzy drinks, wiping his mouth with the back of his hand. "He did good, though. Jamal. Got real good money for all them TVs and stuff. Even split three ways it was more'n what Momma made, and then after the brick I started gettin' a cut, too. Mo told Momma we was workin' down on a farm pickin' strawberries after school. She said she'd come pick too, if the money were that good, but Mo told her no, it was hard work in the sun, and she was better off stayin' inside. She worked at a grocery, I think. Or maybe it was answerin' phones.

"Weren't much longer before she passed. There one day and gone the next. We was snatchin' jewelry by then, too, if somethin' looked nice enough, and I 'member Mo callin' me over to see some necklaces, and askin' which one I thought Momma would like. I picked the blue one, and they put it on her to wear in the coffin. Boy, that made Bad Jack mad. Said it was too good for the likes 'a her, and her bein' dead besides, but Mo just pulled out his switchblade and said he'd cut Bad Jack's head off if he said one more word about Momma. I always wondered if Bad Jack went back later and dug her up to steal it again. I hope not. She deserved somethin' nice in the end."

Fuzzy sits silently, somberly, until his bowels ruin the moment. I open my mouth to remind him, but he's already raising the jug.

"Yeah, yeah, I know, doc. Have a drink. Boy, this really tastes like salt. You want some? It'll go faster if we share."

"It's not for sharing," I say with a sigh. "It's medicine. You have to finish it yourself."

"Now what kind of medicine's made from salt? You ever heard 'a such a thing, Ralph?"

"My doctor says I get too much salt," Ralph says, and Fuzzy points at me accusingly.

"You see? You see, doc? You must've made some kind of mistake."

"Just drink it, Fuzzy."

"Doc Yardley never—"

"Oh, for the love of Christ. Let me out of here," I say to Ralph. "I can't take this anymore."

I pace the hallway outside of Fuzzy's cell, close enough to hear his gastric distress, but far enough away that I don't have to look at him.

"You'd make a lousy prisoner," Ralph says. "You were

only in the box a couple hours."

I jab my finger in Fuzzy's direction, too furious to speak. I've left my medical bag lying in my path, and I nearly trip over it as I make yet another turn. I give it a solid kick and it slides several feet away.

"Don't be too hard on him," Ralph says. "He's had a rough day."

A resounding blast from the cell punctuates the sentiment. Ralph leans over to look through the bars. "You okay, Fuzz?"

The response, if any, is lost in the encore. I sink to the floor with my head in my hands.

"Why don't you head on home?" Ralph says. "I'll watch him, make sure he finishes that stuff. Watching him's what I'm doing anyhow."

"It might not be enough," I mutter. "The loperamide isn't taking effect, and his ass is running like a faucet. How much did he eat?"

"Oh, he went to town, Fuzzy did."

I groan.

"What do you need, doc? Would a coffee fix you up?"

I take off my glasses and rub my eyes. Even out here the smell is awful.

"Wouldn't hurt," I say, and Ralph points me toward the canteen. I drag my medical bag after me and trudge down the hall.

If only I'd left after I gave him the loperamide.

At a quarter to three I convince myself to return to the cell. Fuzzy's still on the can, his gut rumbling away, and he's hardly touched the rehydration solution. He looks tired. Unwell.

His skin is pale and his eyes are closed.

When I take his wrist to check his pulse, he comes alert with all the grace of a bellyflop.

"Wha—oh, it's just you, doc. Thought you left."

"Just needed to stretch my legs." I put a bottle in his hand, a sports drink still cold from the vending machine. "Drink this. It's strawberry lemonade."

"I don't feel good, doc. M'not thirsty."

"You're extremely thirsty, Fuzzy. Drink this."

He raises the bottle to his mouth half-heartedly, failing to realize the cap is still on. I remove it. He takes a sip.

"Strawberry lemonade, huh? Did you make this one too, doc?"

"No."

"Would it hurt your feelings that this one's better?"

"No. Just keep drinking it."

Slowly he drains the bottle, perking up as he does. I ask Ralph to bring another. Fuzzy says, "If they got any blue raspberry, I like that one best."

"Whatever you say, Fuzz," Ralph says. He gives me a nod. I say to Fuzzy, "You still need to finish the other bottle."

"The salty one?"

"Yes."

"It's not as good, doc."

"I'm sorry about that," I say, and he cocks his head at me like he's surprised. I straighten my shirtsleeves and clear my throat. "But it's medicine, and you need to take it. I'm telling you as your doctor."

Fuzzy squints at me, and though he's the one handcuffed to a toilet, emitting sounds and smells no person should ever be witness to, I'm the one who can't sustain eye contact.

"All right, doc," he says at length. "I'll drink it. I'll do this one first before the blue raspberry. Boy, I hope Ralph can find some blue raspberry."

He finishes half the remaining rehydration solution in one long chug. I have to tell him to slow down.

"Can't make up your mind, can you," he says, and belches. "First I ain't drinkin' enough, now I'm drinkin' too much. You sound just like Bad Jack."

"How do you mean?" I ask. I'm merely trying to keep him awake. He has a lot of rehydration still to do.

"Wantin' it both ways. And you can't have it both ways, doc. Mo told me that. Can't have your cake and eat it too, that's what he'd say. I never really knew what that meant. I figure what's the point in havin' cake if you're not gonna eat it? But Mo weren't really talkin' about cake. He were talkin' about the gang.

"After Momma died, things really changed for the ol' Domino Gang. They started stayin' with us, Bad Jack and Tyrone did. Just moved right in. I asked Tyrone about it once, and he said it was 'cuz they liked us so much. I don't know that I believed it, but that's what he said. Mo wouldn't let 'em take our mattresses, though. He said they could sleep on the floor or piss off.

"I 'member wakin' up in the night sometimes, and lookin' across the room at Mo on his mattress. He always put it in front 'a the door so they wouldn't come in without his knowin'. He'd just be sittin' there in the dark, playin' with his switchblade. I 'member that sound it made. *Snick, snick.* It was a nice one, too, with a big long blade and a green stone in the handle. He must've swiped it from a house."

Fuzzy takes another gulp, then makes a face as he endures a particularly rude excretion. He gives me his toothless grin.

"Sorry 'bout that, doc. 'Scuse me a moment."

He flushes the toilet and then continues.

"He took it real hard, Mo did. Momma's death, and Bad Jack and Tyrone movin' in. Made 'im mad. He started pickin' fights with Bad Jack over every little thing. That's when he started talkin' about cake. Can't have your cake and eat it too, he'd say. Can't keep stealin' TVs one at a time and make some real money. Can't pull a big job without the right equipment. He wanted guns, Mo did. Said we couldn't do a big job without guns.

"But Bad Jack was the idea man, and he didn't like Mo's idea, not one bit. See, he'd been in prison before, somewheres in Georgia, and he said he weren't never goin' back. Keep it small-time, he said. That's how you don't get caught. It'll add up, you'll see. But Mo didn't think it was addin' up."

Fuzzy takes another swig, his cheeks ballooning like a bullfrog before he swallows. "That too much, doc? Or not enough?"

"Just right," I say, and Fuzzy grins.

"Now I got it figured out. Always was a slow learner, least that's what Bad Jack said. He said even if it was a sure thing, and even if we had guns, he weren't gonna pull no big job with me. Said I was no good at thinkin' on my feet. I said what about that time I threw the brick through the window, Bad Jack? And I think he woulda hit me again, if it wasn't for Mo.

"Now Mo, he weren't ever a big guy, but then I suppose neither was Bad Jack. And even though he had smarts, Bad Jack didn't have no switchblade. But Mo did, and he flicked it open quick as lightnin' and held it to Bad Jack's throat, and he told 'im that we was a package deal, me and Mo, and not only that, but he was gonna be makin' the decisions from here on out, and if Bad Jack and Tyrone didn't like it, they could split. No more 'a this horseshit, Mo said. He wasn't gonna keep stealin' TVs for the rest 'a his life. He was gonna do one big job and get enough cash to go to Houston, and they could be in or they could be out, but this was the last time he was gonna ask, and this was the last time he wanted t'hear either of 'em talkin' mean about me. He always looked out for me, Mo did. Best big brother a fellow could ask for. You got any kids, doc?"

"One," I say.

"Boy or girl?"

"Girl."

"That's too bad," he says, and his expression is genuinely sorry. "I think every family should start with a boy. That way there's always a big brother. But maybe you could still get one from the 'doption place! I bet they got lots to choose from. Always wondered how that worked, if it's like goin' to the store and tryin' on pants until you find the ones you like, or maybe you gotta take a test or somethin'. How do you reckon they do it, doc?"

I massage my temples. "I haven't the foggiest, Fuzzy."

"The foggiest what, doc?"

"Why don't you have a little more to drink."

He takes another bullfroggy gulp. "Boy, Ralph sure is takin' a long time. I hope he found the blue raspberry. You like blue raspberry, doc?"

"Sure."

"I like that one best. Or watermelon. I shoulda told Ralph that watermelon's good, too. You ever seen a real watermelon, doc? They don't look nothin' like the candy. I never woulda guessed."

Fuzzy releases a low, droning fart. He says, "Mo wanted to work at NASA. Can you believe it? Boy, I can't think of anything worse'n bein' blasted off into outer space. What if they don't bring you back like they was supposed to? What if you got stuck up there? I bet it's dark most 'a the time. I never much liked the dark.

"I asked Mo what I was s'posed to do, if he were with NASA and up in space, and he said he wasn't gonna go to space. I said, then why you wanna work for NASA, Mo? And he said they got people there who do other things. Like buildin' rockets, I said? But Mo said nah, he was gonna work on the computers. I said, why you gotta go to NASA to do that, Mo? Why don't we just steal one? An' Mo laughed and said a computer weren't gonna fit in the van. I said to Mo, I don't know nothin' about computers, Mo, how'm I s'posed to work on them too? And Mo said they got people there who do other things, things I might like better. And he said the money was real good. So that's why we was goin' to NASA.

"But NASA's a long ways away, you know. Mo showed me on a map. It don't really look that far on a map, but you gotta cross three whole states to get there from Florida. Takes a lot 'a money to travel, Mo said, and plus he wanted to get a suit. Said it would make 'im look smart. Hey Ralph! You find the blue raspberry?"

"Sorry, Fuzzy," Ralph says, as he hands another sports drink to me through the bars. "No blue raspberry. But I got you watermelon."

Fuzzy beams.

"First finish the other one," I say, but Fuzzy's already chugging, shaking the last few drops out of the jug. He sets it down triumphantly and holds his hand out for the sports drink. I remove the cap and pass it over. Fuzzy takes a sip, smacking his lips.

"Boy, that's good stuff. How come I ain't never got this before, Ralph? Doc Yardley never gives me nothin' to drink."

"You've never had the shits like this, Fuzz."

"S'pose that's true. You remind me next time, so I don't order that cheesecake. Or maybe I oughta, if it means gettin' some 'a this stuff."

Ralph folds his arms. "I don't know if you can smell yourself anymore, but I'd take it as a personal favor if you didn't. You like that stuff so much, just order that instead. Heck, I'll get it for you myself. Just no more cheesecake, what do you say?"

Fuzzy only grins.

"He's a good guy, ain't he?" Fuzzy says to me. "We known each other for what now, fifteen years?"

"Nineteen," says Ralph.

"Nineteen? Huh. Can't believe it's been that long. Lot 'a them guards come'n go, you know, but Ralph, he's stuck around. Most of 'em I never even known their name. I think there was one called Burns, once. Do you 'member somebody called Burns, Ralph?"

Ralph shakes his head.

"Or maybe it was somethin' else. I 'member him, though. Boy, he was big. I was real scared of 'im, 'cuz he had this scar on his face that made it so his mouth don't shut. He was always walkin' around lookin' like this."

Fuzzy curls his lip up on one side and sneers. I expect it

would look more frightening on someone with all their teeth.

"He weren't much of a talker," Fuzzy says. "Most of 'em really don't talk, 'cept to tell you somethin'. Most of the time they was tellin' me to shut up. Even my lawyers get tired 'a listenin' to me, and I had plenty of them over the years. You been in prison as long as I have, I s'pose that's how it goes.

"We had the same lawyer at first, me and Bad Jack, since we was together when we got pinched. But then somewheres down the line he got somebody new, and then the first one quit, or maybe he's the one who died. But I had a whole bunch of 'em since, and they all tell me the same thing, that they're gonna get me outta here. But they couldn't do it, not a one of 'em. I said it's not their fault, I did it, didn't I, but they kept sayin' that thing about the men. How's it go again, Ralph?"

"Mens rea," Ralph says.

"That's the one. I figured it had to do with me still bein' school-age when we got pinched, so I wasn't really men yet, you know? But that ain't what it means. My new lawyer, Mister Jim, he 'splained it to me again, but I can't 'member it anymore'n I 'member ass-tral pro-jeck-shun. He got two kids now, Mister Jim does. He got a girl like you, doc, but he had the boy first. That's the way to do it, if you ask me. Everybody ought to have a big brother."

Fuzzy sips his watermelon drink. Ralph stifles a yawn. I check the time. It's nearly 5 AM.

"What happened, Fuzzy?" I ask. "What happened on the way to NASA?"

Fuzzy sips again from his watermelon drink. He shifts to the left as he passes gas. He says, "They ain't told you 'bout me, doc?"

I feel my neck flush beneath my collar. "I only had a few minutes with your medical file, and there certainly wouldn't be—"

He holds up a hand. "I ain't accusin' you 'a nothin', doc. Just surprised is all. For a while there it seemed like it was all anybody could talk about, but I s'pose that was a long time ago. Lots happenin' in the world since. Did you know we had a black president? Had 'im twice, wasn't it, Ralph? Boy, that never woulda happened back in my day. I always wondered if Bad Jack knew. Seems like I 'member 'im wantin' to be president, too. Or maybe he meant president of somethin' else. But then I gotta wonder, doc. If you ain't mad at me for what I did, then why was you so mean to me?"

He looks at me, waiting for an answer. I haven't got one. I wish again that I'd left after I gave him the loperamide, if only because it would have spared me from this moment. Vomit and flatulence and diarrhea aside, this is, without a doubt, the most uncomfortable I've been all night.

"I'm sorry, Fuzzy," I say at last. "There was no call for my behavior. I should have had more patience."

Fuzzy tilts his head. "You reckon that woulda helped, doc? Havin' more patients? I'dve thought it'd be even harder havin' more people bein' sick, but..."

He lets out a high-pitched laugh, which is interrupted by a high-pitched fart. He laughs again.

"Say, that's a good one, doc! I get it now, patience and patients! I gotta 'member that for Doc Yardley. Hey Ralph, you ever heard the one about the zebra? 'Bout him askin' God whether he was white with black stripes, or black with white stripes? Now how did that go again..."

I wait restlessly for him to piece together his train of thought, and when he's still silent after a few minutes I say, "You were telling me what happened on the way to NASA, Fuzzy."

"Was I? Sorry doc, I must've forgot. What was I sayin?"

"You and Mo, Fuzzy. You were going to go to NASA, but first you needed—"

"Needed money, yeah, I 'member now. For the trip and for Mo's suit. He thought it'd impress 'em, you know, if he had a suit. So we needed the money, and we needed a big job to get it.

"He had the job all figured, said it would be a cinch. We was gonna hit Big Steve's SoundTracks and Stereos. They sold more'n just stereos, 'a course, they had TVs and electric vacuums and cameras, too. But they was expectin' a big shipment of brand-new stereos and we was gonna make off with that. But first Mo said we needed the guns.

"I 'member I said to Mo, what're we gonna need the guns for, Mo? We're just gonna bust in at night when there ain't nobody there. But Mo said we needed 'em, and he knew best, didn't he? It were his idea, after all.

"So one night we all got in the van, and Mo drove down to the Sears and Roebuck, and Tyrone got to work gettin' us in. He was a real whiz, Tyrone. Real smart with all them 'lectronics, and he could jimmy open any door you wanted. Had this little pouch full'a tools he kept in his pocket all the time. I asked him once if he could show me how he did it, but he pretended like he didn't hear. Tyrone weren't really mean, you know. He just weren't no good at sharin'.

"Once we was inside, Mo showed us all where the guns were, and Tyrone got to work there, too. Mo knew where they was 'cuz he'd already been at the Sears and Roebuck durin' the daytime, scopin' it out. That's how he knew there weren't no security, neither. Least not any guards. Hey Ralph, you know why Sears and Roebuck never had no security guards? They got lots of good stuff in there."

"No idea, Fuzzy," Ralph says. "That was a long time ago."

"They got lots of good stuff in there," Fuzzy says to me. "Clothes 'n shoes 'n jewelry 'n such. They had a bunch 'a 'lectronics, too. I said to Mo, hey Mo, why don't we just take these 'lectronics instead 'a the ones from Big Steve? But Mo said that wasn't the plan. It was important we stick to the plan, he said. But boy did they have some good stuff.

"I was lookin' around, you know, just seein' what they had while we was waitin' on Tyrone. I coulda used some new shoes, or maybe a new jacket or somethin'. But then I saw the perfume counter. You ever seen a perfume counter, doc? I couldn't stop lookin' at it. All them little bottles, and they was all lit up. Looked so pretty. I figured they was meant for women, but then what's the harm in just smellin'? I never smelled a woman before."

Fuzzy takes a sip of his watermelon drink, shaking his head mournfully.

"I just thought it was stuck, doc. I didn't mean to break it. I just thought the door was stuck. But next thing I know the glass is broke, and the 'larm's goin' off and Bad Jack is yellin', and then I was yellin' too for Tyrone to make it stop, and that's when I saw Mo's face. I knew I'd done it then, doc. I knew I messed up bad.

"Mo started yellin' for Tyrone and Bad Jack to grab the guns, and he yelled for me to go out'n start the van. So that's what I did, and that's when I heard them police sirens. Boy, they sure came fast, doc. Didn't know they could come so fast. I left the van runnin' and I went lickety-split back inside, and I told 'em you gotta hurry up, fellas, the police is almost here. And we all went runnin' outside together.

"They was just pullin' up, the police officers, and they seen what we got. They started yellin' too, sayin' for us to drop the weapons, put 'em up, you know, all that police stuff. You ever seen the police in real life, doc? It's scarier than on TV. Boy, I was scared. I coulda shit a brick."

Fuzzy pauses as he shits something significantly less substantial, then reaches over his shoulder to flush the toilet.

"I didn't have no gun," he says, "on account of I went to start the van, so I didn't have nothin' to drop. I just put my hands up like this and started screamin' don't shoot, don't shoot!"

Fuzzy reaches for the ceiling, his sports drink sloshing.

"Tyrone, he put his guns down right away, and Bad Jack, he was so busy yellin' I don't think he even heard what he was s'posed to do. But Mo, he just stood there, starin' at the police, and he was holdin' a gun too. They was yellin' for him to put it down and I was sayin' too put it down Mo, put it down, 'cuz they was aimin' for him. But he wouldn't put it down. And then they started shootin'."

Fuzzy's eyes go hard, his hand tightening around the bottled sports drink, his toothless mouth working up and down.

"I 'member it like it were yesterday. Nobody ain't never believed me, but I was there, and I still 'member it just the way it happened. They shot at 'im first, they did. The police, they shot at 'im first. So when Mo shot back it were only in self-defence. He was just protectin' hisself, and me besides, 'cuz I didn't have no gun.

"There was two cops, I 'member, and Mo shot the one who was on the left. The other one was hidin' behind the door, you know, the door 'a the car, and he shot Mo 'fore Mo could get 'im. I 'member Mo fallin' to the ground, and I 'member shakin' his shoulders and slappin' 'im in the head, but he wouldn't get up. That cop killed 'im, he did. He killed my brother.

"He was still shootin', that cop, and now Tyrone was shootin' back. He'd picked up one 'a the guns he put down and he was shootin' at the cop. But the cop got 'im too, and then it was just me'n Bad Jack.

"I saw Bad Jack runnin' for the van, which was sorta in between us'n the cop, you know? So I ran for it too. Bad Jack was screamin' 'bout never going back to prison, and he was shootin' at the cop too, but that cop, boy, he musta been lucky or somethin', 'cuz Bad Jack couldn't hit 'im neither. But he was still shootin' at us, and Bad Jack was busy shootin' back, and so I was the one who was drivin'.

"I weren't really a good driver, didn't have no permit or nothin', but we was in a pinch, so I just did my best. That's when the cop came outta his hidin' spot, shootin' at the van, and I just turned the wheel and went for 'im. Knocked 'im right down. Bad Jack was yellin' for me to hit 'im again, so that's what I did. Ran 'im over again and again, till his guts was spilled out and his head was popped like a grape. I was so busy runnin' 'im over that I didn't even see the other cops, not until we was surrounded, and by then it was too late. We was caught."

Fuzzy farts for a good twenty seconds, wrinkling his nose.

"It just keeps comin', don't it? Sorry 'bout all this, doc. I weren't expectin' to be around for this part."

I'm still reconciling shootouts and heads like popped grapes with the man I see before me. It's a moment before I register what he's said.

"What do you mean, you weren't expecting to be around?"

He cocks his head at me. "Ain't you know this is death row?"

"Well, sure, I mean, I suppose, but..."

Oh.

Oh.

"Say doc, is it true that you can still break wind even after you're dead? Boy, wouldn't that be somethin'. How long after, do you reckon? You think it's just for a little while, or does it last—"

I bolt off the cot, hastening for the cell door.

"Let me out of here," I say, my voice straining. "Please. Just let me out."

Ralph brings me a sports drink from the vending machine. Watermelon. I sit in the hallway with my back against the wall.

"They didn't tell you," Ralph says. He takes the cap off and hands me the bottle. I can't even look at it. I push it away.

"He knew it was coming," Ralph says. "He's been waiting to die for most of his life."

"But he's afraid of needles," I say, as if that means anything.

Ralph nods. "That's why he's going in Old Sparky."

I bury my face in my hands. "Jesus Christ."

"Lucked out tonight, he did," Ralph says. "Got a last-minute stay. Bad Jack was up first, and something went wrong.

That's why Doc Yardley's tied up. Fuzzy'll probably get another few months out of it before the death warrant comes through again. Get another last meal out of it, too. He was really looking forward to it the first time around. All he talked about for weeks."

I can only shake my head. I've been awake all night, and right now it all just seems like too much. Ralph leans against the wall beside me.

"You're a young fella, doc. Still new to the game, I expect. You can't—"

"Can't save them all?" I mutter, but Ralph sort of huffs. I look up. He says, "You can't look at it as either or, because it's not. It's both, and it always will be. You get it?"

"No," I mutter. Ralph chuckles.

"You will, son. Now, if you aren't gonna drink that, I know somebody who will."

Ralph lets me back into the cell and I give Fuzzy the drink. His face lights up.

"Boy, this is my lucky day. Thanks, doc." He slurps back half of it and wipes his mouth. "Hey doc, I just realized I never even asked you your name."

Fuzzy looks at me expectantly. His lips are tinged pink from the coloring in the drinks. He cracks a smile, revealing five rosy teeth.

"It's Evergreen," I say. "My name is Evergreen."

Fuzzy sets down the sports drink and sticks out his hand. After a moment's consideration, I shake it.

"Well, I sure am pleased to meet you, Doc Evergreen. Say, I forgot to ask you earlier, but I got this tickle in my throat, and I heard somethin' 'bout a virus..."

"I'm sure it's nothing to be concerned about," I say, but when his face falls I unlatch my bag. "Of course, I'd be happy to take a look."

"Thanks, doc. I sure appreciate it. Hey! I just 'membered the rest of that joke! Hey Ralph! You wanna hear the one about the zebra?"

"Go ahead, Fuzz," Ralph says with a smile.

Fuzzy turns to me. "So this zebra, he's not sure which one he is, you know, if he's white with black stripes or if he's black with white stripes, so he asks his friend. I can't 'member what the friend is, I think he's a hippo, or maybe a lion, but it don't really matter I don't think. But the hippo don't know, either, so he tells the zebra to climb up the mountain an' ask God.

"The hippo's waitin' at the bottom of the mountain for 'im, and when the zebra comes down he asks, so what did God say? And the zebra tells 'im God just said you are what you are, and the poor zebra's still lookin' confused.

"That must mean you're white with black stripes, the hippo says, and the zebra says, well how do you know that? And the hippo says, 'cuz if you was black with white stripes, God woulda told you you is what you is!"

Fuzzy slaps his knee, laughing so hard his eyes are watering. "You get it? You get it, doc? Boy, it's a good thing I never told that to Bad Jack. He'dve knocked the rest of my teeth out!"

He pounds his leg, doubling over, laughing hysterically. Ralph starts to chuckle. Before I know it, I'm laughing too.

"You get it, doc?" Fuzzy manages between gasps. "You get it?"

I locate my otoscope and snap on a fresh tip. My own eyes

are watering. I can't help but smile.

"Yes, Fuzzy. I believe I do."

* * *

This story first appeared in the After Dinner Conversation—July 2021 issue.

Discussion Questions

1. Fuzzy is made out to be a likable character who killed a police officer when he was underage. Does any of that matter regarding his punishment? Should he have gotten the death penalty, life in prison, or some other punishment?

2. Given his upbringing, and the influence of his surroundings and his brother Mo, did Fuzzy have any real choices in life that could have led him on another path? Does that matter regarding his punishment?

3. Should a "cop killer" ever be treated with respect and dignity? Can a person commit a crime so terrible that they are never worthy of respect and dignity?

4. Does the relative level of education of Fuzzy have any bearing on his culpability in the crimes and death he committed? What would have been required to turn the Domino gang around to useful members of society?

5. What is the purpose of the judicial system, to punish, to deter, or to reform? Do different variations in crime and age require different answers to the previous question, or is the answer always the same?

* * *

Conveyor

Ciaran McCarthy

* * *

I'm sitting upright in a chair in a bright, white room that makes me think of a clinic. I don't know where I am nor how I got here. Two people, strangers, stand in front of me. One is wearing a pale blue uniform with a yellow badge on his chest. He steps forward.

"Arthur Montague?" he says.

I tell him, "I don't know who that is."

He sighs. "C'mon Montague. Don't draw this out for longer than it has to be."

He must be mistaking me for someone else, for I've never heard of that name before in my life. My name is... and I realize that I cannot remember. All my memories from before are gone. What is happening here? I look at the other person in front of me. This one is wearing a sharp gray suit. He's holding a folder close to his chest. His face is unreadable.

"This sometimes happens," says a third person. I can only see her head and shoulders as she's sitting behind a device with many cables flowing out of it in different directions. A finger twirls through her long hair. She is the youngest of the three.

"But that's him, right?" says Blue Uniform.

"Oh yeah, that's him, all right."

Long Hair stands up and comes to me. She starts carefully removing cables that are attached to little pads, which in turn are suckered to my hands, my forearms, my face. They make tiny popping sounds, and I think of leeches. I start ripping them off too. "Don't break them," chides Long Hair. I console myself with the fact that I'm fully clothed, albeit in a shabby brown suit that must have had several owners before me. Then Long Hair removes a strange kind of hat that was on my head. It's made of metal and covered in a web of little blue wires. I hadn't noticed it was there until she removed it. I run my hands through my hair, then over my face. Long Hair holds a small mirror in front of me.

"See anyone you recognize?" she asks.

The face I see is middle-aged and healthy, though gray has started creeping into the brown hair. It has green eyes.

Is this me, I wonder. I shake my head.

"Don't worry. Your memories should return soon," says Long Hair.

Gray Suit clears his throat. "Mr. Montague, I am your defense attorney. Your trial will start shortly and should take no longer than half an hour. By law, I'm required to provide you with a statement of the charges against you, as well as a summary of the evidence to be presented."

He hands me the folder. I want to read it immediately, but Gray Suit says, "We must go now. Please follow me. Thanks, Clarissa."

This is apparently Long Hair's name. She gives him a friendly smile and continues to gather up the cables. I don't understand what's happening, and my memories still haven't returned, but there's little I can do here. I decide to go along with them until I can figure out what's going on.

My legs are stiff, weak, and I stand a little unsteadily. Blue Uniform takes my arm, and the three of us walk down a narrow corridor. It's dimly lit, but the door at the end is outlined by a bright light coming from within. The only noise is our footsteps on the tiled floor. Suddenly I think of churches, of holy places, of hellfire, and I feel an overpowering sense of dread coming from inside that door. I stagger backward; Blue Uniform holds me and jostles me forward.

At the door, Gray Suit asks, "Ready?" and then opens it without waiting for my reply. The light dazzles me for a moment; then I come to see that it's a near-empty courtroom. I'm led to a desk near the front. Almost directly before me is a projector screen. At another desk, twin to mine, is a short woman in a green dress suit. She gives me a sour look, and I dislike her immediately. The judge, waiting at his dais to the front, is more to my liking. There is an air of elderly wisdom about him that puts me at ease. He'll set right whatever's going on here.

He bangs his gavel half-heartedly. "The Supreme Court of the Second Republic is now in session." To my horror, he sounds bored by these proceedings, as though he has done this a thousand times already. He turns to me. "Arthur Montague, you are charged with the following: mass murder, ethnic cleansing, genocide, use of biological weapons, use of chemical weapons, crimes against peace, and crimes against humanity.

How do you plead?"

What is this? Biological and chemical weapons? Genocide? And my plea—surely, I'm not being accused of *this*? I look at Gray Suit; he's my defense attorney, he'll speak up against this madness. But instead, he gives me a short nod.

"I don't understand," I tell the judge. My voice squeaks like a little creature. I swallow and try again. "I don't remember..."

"Not guilty," says the judge over me. He turns now to Sour Woman. "Prosecution, please present your case."

"Thank you, Judge. We request that the video be played."

The lights are dimmed. The projector screen turns blue, then the video plays. It begins with scenes of airplanes flying in formation. Bombs cascading from them like raindrops. Towns burning. Thick plumes of smoke from ruins. Soldiers firing into a crowd. People running. People screaming. People falling. Bodies lying across the streets, the fields, half-buried in the rubble of a destroyed building. Roads pocked from shelling. Doctors and patients in a makeshift hospital. One of them is a woman lying on a bed. Her face is completely white, and her eyelids flutter. She could be twenty or seventy. Other patients appear. Some are missing limbs. Some are missing eyes. An elderly man has a burn across his face and down the side of his body. Then there's a cloud of white gas, viewed from above. It flows through a city, creeping along the streets, silently engulfing buildings. Mass graves. When the children come, I look away.

Gray Suit hisses in my ear, "No, you have to watch."

I brave another look at the video; now it shows a gentleman with brown hair, kind green eyes, and a happy smile.

I recognize his face from the mirror held by Long Hair. He's sitting at a long table with a group of generals, examining a map. Next, he is giving a rousing speech in a public square. Then he is sitting at a grand desk inside an opulent room, signing documents before the video returns to the same horrors as before. The video ends with a still of the man with the caption: ARTHUR MONTAGUE. PRESIDENT OF THE FIRST REPUBLIC.

The lights come back on. Sour Woman says, "Judge, the prosecution rests."

"Thank you. The defense may now present its case, if it has one this time."

They all stare at me. I look again to my defense attorney, willing him to say something, but he's completely unmoved. I'm completely helpless. Everyone seems to know what's going on, but no one has told me.

"I don't remember any of that," I wave at the projector screen, that portal into hell. "That wasn't me..."

At last, Gray Suit rouses himself! "The re-creation process can be like this, Judge. Sometimes he remembers things immediately. Other times it takes a few hours. He was re-created just before the trial began. It's not unusual for him not to remember anything."

"But he was re-created correctly? This *is* Arthur Montague?"

Gray Suit smiles at me. "Oh yes, this is most certainly him."

"Sometimes," the judge says, not addressing anyone in particular, "sometimes, I wonder about the wisdom of doing this over and over again. Every week we've re-created him, put him on trial, and sentenced him. Every week, for the past sixty years. Next week, we will do it again. I ask myself: what purpose does it still serve...?"

Sour Woman stands up suddenly: "You're not the only one who wonders that, Judge. There are a lot of us who think this show trial has lost all meaning. Even now, decades after he was first executed, Montague still consumes so much of our time and attention. He needs to die once and for all."

There is a long silence in the courtroom before Gray Suit says, "Perhaps, Judge, this is a question for another time?"

The judge looks weary but says, "Quite. For now, if the defense has no case to present, I will render my verdict."

"But I didn't do anything!" I protest.

The judge dons a black cap. "Arthur Montague, the Supreme Court of the Second Republic finds you guilty on all charges brought before it. Due to the nature of your crimes, I sentence you to death. Your sentence will take place immediately. Court is adjourned."

He bangs his gavel. I say, "I don't—" but it is already too late. The judge is leaving the courtroom. Sour Woman is gathering up her papers. I turn to Gray Suit.

He says, "Twenty-two minutes. That was quicker than I was expecting. Now for the final act, Mr. Montague."

Blue Uniform grabs my arm and pulls me through another door into a different corridor. The evidence folder falls, unread, from my hand, and I don't have time to retrieve it. At a division in the corridor, Gray Suit stops.

"This is where we part, Mr. Montague. Someone else is scheduled to be your defense attorney next week. Or your re-creation's, to be precise. I've lost count of how many times I've told you this, and you won't remember anyway, but my mother was ten when you bombed the town of Callinaugh with nerve gas. She was lucky to escape. My grandparents and uncle did not. It gives me the greatest pleasure to know that a monster like you will face justice today, and next week, and the week after that, and the week after that. And I hope you suffer. For every. Single. Moment."

He punches me in the jaw before adding, "Goodbye, Mr. Montague," and marching down one direction. Blue Uniform drags me along the other. We climb a flight of stairs to a door with a semi-opaque window. Through it is the outside, and I find myself on top of a metal balcony. In the middle is a steel gallows. The trapdoor underneath is bordered in yellow and black stripes with a lever nearby. When I see the wire noose, I attempt to flee back down the stairs, but Blue Uniform grabs me around the waist and throws me to the floor. The balcony rattles underneath me.

"Now, now, there's no need for that," says a new voice. I can't tell if it's addressing me or Blue Uniform. I'm pulled up to my feet and come face-to-face with a stocky man with plump red cheeks and watery eyes.

"Good morning, Mr. Montague. I'm Henry, your executioner. Always a pleasure to meet you. Oh, I am sorry; I don't mean to be so cavalier. We've been here... how many times now? You won't remember me, though. They tell me you only get back your pre-trial memories."

I catch sight of the noose, gently twisting in the breeze.

"Mr. Montague?"

"I'm sorry, what?"

"I asked if you had any questions, Mr. Montague."

I look around, wondering if there's anything I could say that would save me. The balcony overlooks a concrete yard. There doesn't seem to be anyone else around. It is a cold, gray day. Everything is quiet.

"No one here to watch, I'm afraid," says Henry, as though reading my thoughts. "For years after they first brought you back, they charged admittance. That's how much people wanted to see you die. But I guess you're not as famous as you used to be. We still get the occasional school group, but that's about it. If you could just step this way, please, sir."

I take a step onto the trapdoor, and my legs give way. Then I find I can't move them. Henry is speaking, but I cannot hear. I feel like I'm drowning. Images from the video come back to me. A cloud of poison gas. My smiling face. The children.

Both Blue Uniform and Henry hoist me back up again. "Just one step at a time, sir, if you would."

I find my voice at last. "But I didn't do any of that!" My anguish echoes around the empty courtyard. "That wasn't me! I don't remember any of it! I don't even know where Callinaugh is!"

"Was." Blue Uniform spits on the ground. Henry looks at me with at least some pity but says, "Can't do anything about it now, sir. You've had your trial. Now please hold still. I have to fit this."

He slips the noose over my head and tightens it. It's cold against my neck.

Henry says, "Don't worry, sir. I understand it's just like falling asleep." Then he whispers to me, "Personally, sir, if you were to come back, I'd vote for you. This country could do with someone strong in charge again."

I gaze out over the courtyard, willing my final few seconds to last as long as possible. I try to remember everything: my breathing, the feeling of the noose, the rattle of the balcony as I shift my weight from foot to foot. A bird starts singing. In my head, I say to myself *I am not Arthur Montague and I did not do anything. I am not Arthur Montague and I did not do anything*. White poison gas drifting through a town. The children. *I am not Arthur Montague and I didn't do anything. I'm not Arthur Montague and I—*

"Godspeed, sir," says Henry from behind me. The metal lever clanks, and I fall asleep.

I wake up, and...

* * *

This story first appeared in the After Dinner Conversation—July 2023 issue.

Discussion Questions

1. If you were in charge of this society, what would you do with Arthur Montague at this point? Would you continue to put him on trial and to death over and over again? Would you let him die or let him live out the remainder of his life? Something else?

2. If putting a murderer to death is an appropriate punishment, why isn't it appropriate to put a thousand-time murderer to death a thousand times? What is the purpose of criminal punishment?

3. Should they have waited for Arthur Montague's memory to return before putting him on trial? Should criminals with no memory of the crime they committed ever be put on trial?

4. Is there any limit, of any kind, to the types of punishments permissible for the most unimaginable mass criminal actions?

5. Is the purpose of criminal punishment to create a world without crime? How does your answer to this question shape the types of permissible punishments?

* * *

Soon The Sentence Sign

David M. Hoenig

* * *

Jason Sweeney sat quietly, his hands secured behind him. He glanced at the young uniformed Korean woman who had arrested him.

Marshal Hwang Min Pak didn't so much as look up from her pad and stylus. She clicked a corner of her electronic device, consulted its clock function, then powered it down and put it away. "It's nearly noon local time. We should get to the security tower in another five minutes, give or take, so let me clue you in, given it's your first offense."

Sweeney hunched his shoulders submissively and remained silent.

Marshal Pak settled back in her seat. "Titan's the new frontier, Sweeney Todd. We don't have enough population—or criminals—to warrant a full-time legal system. Circuit court judges have a long haul to get here via interplanetary, so waiting for a regular trial can mean being imprisoned for a long time before anything happens."

The transport began to slow. "But it was just a bar fight, and he started it!"

"I got your statement already, so shut up and listen." Pak put her hand on her prisoner's shoulder and gave a minute squeeze. "You're not such a bad guy, but we caught you, literally, red-handed after slashing someone with a broken bottle. In an illegal establishment. You both broke the law: he's got his process to deal with, and you've got yours." She checked her pad again. "In a very little bit, you'll have some choices to make. You have the right to a trial, so you can either eat survival rations in solitary confinement while you wait for a human judge to get out here, or use the latest AI judicial package approved by Titan Corporation's 'legal beagles'."

Sweeney put his head in his hands. "Great choices."

"Take some advice?" Marshal Pak smiled when he looked at her. The transport slowed to a halt. "Life's too short. Don't wait for a circuit judge. If you're found guilty, you'll end up paying for your own prison sentence in addition to everything else."

"Shit."

"I've worked with Judicial Suite myself, and it's pretty comprehensive. And fair. I've seen cases where all charges were dropped because the AI personality matrices found someone innocent."

"Really?"

"Yeah, but the charges for attorneys, procedures, and all the legal stuff can really rack up, and..."

"And I'm responsible for it if eventually found guilty."

Pak nodded.

"But I could argue my case and go free?"

"I've seen it, Sweeney. But it's probably best to just plead guilty and take the summary judgment from the AI."

"Let a computer decide my fate?"

She snorted laughter.

"What's so funny?"

"Ever since they started holding trials, Sweeney, *someone* decides the guilt or innocence of an accused. You think humans can do it better than artificial intelligence?"

Sweeney considered that.

The transport stopped, and the door slid open. Marshal Pak escorted him into the security, recorded his thumbprint at processing, and took him to an elevator. They went down several levels, and she stopped him at a door. It opened for her, and Sweeney saw a screen and a chair in an otherwise tiny, bare metal room. She took off the cuffs. "In you go."

"What do I do?"

"The computer will explain everything. All you have to do is make choices." She pushed him gently.

Sweeney went into the cubicle without resisting, and the door closed behind him. He sat in the chair.

The screen promptly powered on, and a computerized voice spoke from it. *"Jason A. Sweeney: you have been arrested on charges of assault and battery, assault with a deadly weapon, and public intoxication with an illegal substance."*

"I was drinking in a bar and defended myself from an idiot!"

"Outbursts will not be tolerated: additional charges of contempt of court may be brought against you if you continue in such fashion. This court has reviewed relevant evidence and testimony. Do you contest any of the previously described charges?"

Sweeney blew out a breath before responding. "Yes, all of them."

"If you are not prepared to accept summary judgment from this court for the specified charges, you have the right to either be remanded to solitary confinement on subsistence diet for an unspecified period to await the arrival of a Solar Court-approved judge or to proceed with immediate trial utilizing Judicial Suite 3.7.1 software."

Two icons lit up on the screen, and Sweeney tapped the one on the right. The display cleared.

"Thank you for selecting the use of Judicial Suite 3.7.1. Please indicate if you would like to accept summary judgment based on current evidence or if you would prefer to undergo a virtual trial using this software."

"Question: what exactly does 'summary judgment' mean in this case?"

"It would mean that you acknowledge your guilt on all charges and accept the judgment of this court in assigning an appropriate sentence."

"Hell with that. I want the trial."

"Thank you for choosing to undergo a trial. Judicial Suite 3.7.1 is currently being loaded into the local system... Judge 4.0 has successfully loaded... Jury 2.7 has successfully loaded... Prosecutor 3.1.5 has successfully loaded. Please indicate if you would prefer an AI defense attorney or to represent yourself. Judicial Package 3.7.1 and Titan Corporation strongly recommend selecting the AI Defense attorney."

"Yeah, I want the lawyer."

"Thank you for choosing the AI Defense attorney option. Please peruse the complete collection of AI Defense attorney personalities available to choose from and their costs."

He began scrolling. "You've got to be kidding; there's over eighty different choices!"

"Indeed. Judicial Suite 3.7.1 offers the closest approximation to the ideal of human legal systems, including a multitude of matrices to allow the accused as much latitude as possible."

"Great. Who, or what, is a 'Johnny Cochran?'"

"Specific characteristics, as well as relative strengths and weaknesses of particular personalities in pursuing this proceeding, can be accessed as subheadings under each entry. Once again, Judicial Suite 3.7.1 advises against representing yourself."

"But if I choose an AI, I'm kind of just choosing you, aren't I?"

"No. For each aspect of this case, you will select a unique, specific personality matrix to represent the usual participants in this trial."

Sweeney rubbed his temples. "I really don't understand how you can be you, a judge, opposing lawyers..."

"Historically, the uncertainty of many factors affected the outcome of trials: personal biases of a particular judge assigned to the case, the quality of attorney available, the specific persons selected to the jury. To accurately simulate this exhaustively comprehensive process, accused persons must be provided with the opportunity to make choices and allow for random probabilities which will affect the trial's outcome and, if you are found guilty, the sentencing phase. Your choices will facilitate the exacting and complex legal process of a trial."

"Well, how am I supposed to know what to choose?"

"I can provide you with legal advice based on a cost-value scale, or if you prefer to employ a randomization algorithm for any category..."

Sweeney interrupted. "Can I go back?"

"Specify."

"What happens if we just forget about the trial, and I choose summary judgment instead?"

The computer's response was delayed enough that Sweeney thought that it might have been offended. *"Judicial Suite 3.7.1 is prepared to accept your plea of 'guilty' and to pass sentence based on a median level of punishment for similar crimes across the spectrum of human criminal proceedings. Such a sentence will be moderated by the personal circumstances of the defendant and commensurate with the cost-savings to Titan Corporation that would be realized through avoidance of a lengthy trial."*

Sweeney thought back to the advice that Marshal Pak had given him and carefully touched the "Cancel" icon at the bottom right of the screen. "Fine; I accept summary judgment instead of trial." After just a second, he added, "Please."

"Excellent. In light of the evidence and your cooperation in this proceeding, this court sentences you to a fine of 10 percent of your wages for the next three hundred days, abstinence from intoxicating substances for the same period as documented by biomonitor, and mandatory psychiatric evaluation and attendance/participation with all medically recommended therapy. If you fail in any part of these requirements, you will be immediately sentenced to execution by being exposed to the outside environment. Please agree to all terms of this sentence by thumbprint on the screen."

Jason Sweeney exhaled and applied his thumb to the screen. The cubicle door clicked open.

"Hey." Hwang Min Pak smiled at him from the doorway.

"Is... is that it?"

"Yep. I can get you processed if you're ready."

"What are you still doing here?"

She shrugged. "I made a bet with myself. Wanted to see

how it turned out."

Sweeney stood. "How'd you do?"

"Won it." She smiled. "Each of us in Security had to play through a scenario with Judicial Suite during training."

"Really? Seems like an ugly way to treat an employee."

"Officially, the Corp was testing it for bugs and flexibility, but I'm pretty sure they wanted us to know what it was like."

"Because then you could give someone advice before..."

Her answering grin was wide. "You're not as dumb as you looked back in Dome Eight. C'mon. I already told you, life's too short for this shit."

* * *

This story first appeared in the After Dinner Conversation—March 2021 issue.

Discussion Questions

1. If you were arrested for a crime you knew you committed, would you plead guilty and admit your wrongdoing, or would you force the State to prove your guilt? Why?

2. If you were arrested for a crime you knew you committed, but you knew the government could not prove it, would you plead guilty and admit your wrongdoing anyway? Why? Does your answer change with the nature of the crime? Why?

3. Would you feel comfortable having an AI judge? An AI lawyer? Are there professions where you would prefer AI or a person? What is it about a person, or AI that is compelling in certain situations?

4. The AI system in the story takes into account the cost avoidance saved by pleading guilty *(rather than going to trial)* when determining the punishment; should cost avoidance be a consideration in the justice system?

5. If the narrator had gone to trial, he would have had the choice to pick between different AI lawyers to represent him, each with their own strengths. Do you think it is fair that different lawyers of different quality represent different criminals? If you think it is not fair, what (*if anything*) would be a better system of equal legal defense?

* * *

Bunny Racing (Children's Story)

Tyler W. Kurt

* * *

In the land of rabbits, there were two young bunny rabbits, Hopper and Bounce, and they were the very best of friends. Hopper and Bounce played together almost every day and did the usual things that bunnies did, like scrunch their noses, and scratch their ears, but their favorite thing to do was run.

They ran everywhere they went together and because they ran all time, they got faster and faster. Sometimes they would race each other, but they were almost exactly the same speed, so it was almost always a tie.

One day they were running in a field when an older rabbit saw them and said, "Dang, you two are the fastest bunnies I have ever seen, maybe the fastest bunnies in the world. You two should enter the Rabbit Racing Championships!" Hopper and Bounce's eyes immediately lit up with excitement.

"I'm going to be the fastest rabbit in the race!" said Hopper.

"You mean the second fastest rabbit," Bounce said jokingly, "because you are going to be right behind me!"

Well, they did go to the race, and it was a huge race! There were more rabbits there to watch the race than Hopper or Bounce had ever seen in one place in their entire lives. And there were rabbits there to race, too! Tall rabbits, short rabbits, brown rabbits, white rabbits. Rabbits with big ears, and rabbits with small ears. Rabbits of every shape and size.

Well, pretty soon it was time to start, so Hopper and Bounce lined up with the other rabbits. Then the announcer yelled, "Go!"

Hopper and Bounce were fast, and within just a few strides they were already leading the race.

They ran through a field of tall brown grass where they could hardly see, then through a dried-out riverbed. Then over a beautiful field of short green grass that felt soft on their rabbit feet.

"We are... going to... win!" Hopper said to Bounce, through heavy breathing. But just as he said that he saw three other rabbits, led by a rabbit with a bent ear, coming up behind them, gaining ground. Thump, thump. Thump, thump.

"We... have to... run... faster!" yelled Bounce. But there was no hope. Bent Ear and his two friends ran past Hopper and Bounce. Bent Ear went on to win the race, and Hopper and Bounce came in fourth and fifth place.

"They were... so fast," Hopper said, still out of breath. "They must run all the time. I'm going to hop over to them, and talk to them, and learn everything they have to teach me." And that's exactly what he did.

A year later, Hopper and Bounce were back at the race ready to try to win again. This time, however, just as they were heading to the starting line, Hopper pulled Bounce by the ear into a nearby bush.

"What are you doing!" screamed Bounce. "That's my ear you're pulling on!"

Hopper looked around to make sure no other rabbits were looking, and then pulled out a very strange carrot. "This," said Hopper, "is what Bent Ear and his friends were eating before the race last year that made them so fast."

"What is it?" asked Bounce.

"It's a special carrot from the forbidden forest—"

"—the forbidden forest!" shouted Bounce, "But no bunny is allowed in the forbidden forest, because it's so dangerous!"

"I know," said Hopper, "But they went there, so I went there. I know I broke the rules, but it made me really mad that they beat us last year. So, when they told me what they did, I did it, too."

"But that's cheating," said Bounce.

"Look," said Hopper. "We both know we are the fastest rabbits out here. The only reason Bent Ear and his friends beat us is because they ate these special carrots from the forbidden forest before the race. So, if we eat them too, we aren't getting a special advantage, we are just making everything equal again. So, it's not really cheating." Hopper started eating his special carrot and handed Bounce the other special carrot for him to eat.

What Hopper said made sense. If everyone was eating the special carrots, then maybe it wasn't really cheating? Bounce looked at the special carrot Hopper was holding out for him and he was thinking about eating it, but then his stomach started to feel like two butterflies were dancing in it. Something inside made Bounce feel like eating the special carrot was wrong.

"No," Bounce said, "I think I'd rather just run on my own."

"Okay," Hopper said, "suit yourself."

Not too much later, the race started and, just like the year before, Hopper and Bounce started off faster than all the other rabbits. "See," Bounce said to Hopper, "I told you I didn't need the special carrot!"

And, just like last year, they ran through a field of tall brown grass, then through a dried-out riverbed, and then over a beautiful field of short green grass that felt soft on their rabbit feet.

But, just like the year before, when Bounce looked back, he saw Bent Ear and his friends gaining ground on them. Thump, thump. Thump, thump. Bounce turned to Hopper to yell "Run faster!" but when he looked around, Hopper was already far out in front of him. The special carrot was working.

Bounce ran as fast as his rabbit feet could carry him, but Hopper was even faster. Just like the year before, Bent Ear and his friends ran past Bounce. But not only that, the other rabbits passed Bounce, too. "The secret is out," thought Bounce, "everyone is eating the special carrots but me!"

In the end, Hopper won the race, and Bounce finished dead last.

This went on for five years, which is a very long time in rabbit years. And in all five years Hopper and the other rabbits would eat their special carrots before the race. And in all five years Hopper came in first place, and Bounce came in dead last.

Well, no bunny had ever won the race five years in a row, so Hopper became very famous. At least, famous for a rabbit. All the other rabbits knew him by name, and they all admired him. Nobody admired Bounce.

In fact, Hopper was so important, and so famous, that he had lots of new rabbit friends. He had so many new friends that Hopper hardly ever had time to spend with Bounce anymore. And this made Bounce sad, and maybe just a little bit jealous.

Hopper used his new rabbit fame to help other rabbits that needed help too. Like, one time, when a rabbit lost his bushy tail to a coyote, Hopper used his fame to get all the other rabbits to collect cotton from the fields. He then gave the cotton to the tail-less rabbit so he could put the cotton on its behind where its tail used to be. Of course, a cotton tail isn't as good as a real tail, but it's better than no tail at all.

Finally, in the sixth year, after coming in last place again, Bounce just couldn't take it anymore and he yelled out at the finish line, as loud as he could, "They are all cheating, every bunny is cheating. They are all eating special carrots from the forbidden forest!"

The crowd went quiet. The old rabbit who was in charge of the race, whose fur had turned gray with age, came up to Hopper and the other rabbits and asked, "Is that true?" But he could tell by the guilty look on Hopper's face that it was.

"Yes, it's true," said Hopper. "But I wanted so badly to win, and everybody else was eating the special carrots, so doesn't that make us all equal?"

"I'm not eating the special carrots!" said Bounce.

"Well maybe you should!" snapped Hopper. "I tried to tell

you to eat them, but your pride wouldn't let you! Look at the all the good I've done by being famous! I have helped so many other bunnies that needed help! If you take this all away, I won't be famous, and I won't be able to help other rabbits that need help. Also," said Hopper, "I won't be able to win the race anymore."

The old rabbit thought a long time. Both Bounce and Hopper had made good points. But finally, the old rabbit decided what to do ...

* * *

This story first appeared in the After Dinner Conversation—December 2020 issue.

Discussion Questions

1. Is Hopper right? If everyone is eating the special carrots, is it really cheating?
2. Does it matter that the only way to get the special carrots is by breaking the rules and going into the forbidden forest?
3. Does Hopper doing good things with his fame make up for the fact that he was eating the special carrots from the forbidden forest?
4. Did Bounce really tell on Hopper and the others because he was angry they were cheating, or because he was angry he was losing?
5. Should Hopper and Bounce remain friends after all this over?
6. What do you think the old rabbit should do?

* * *

The Only Punishment

Ville V. Kokko

* * *

The floor of the room was white, but three of the walls and the ceiling were light blue. His own bland pajamas were light green.

It was probably supposed to be calming, but it only angered Rats. He knew what this was—a fregging brainwashing facility, that's what. It didn't matter how *nice* they were trying to be. It was just a part of it.

He glanced angrily at the glass wall. It was the only window in the room, made of thick and unbreakable glass, and it showed nothing but a garden, so overgrown it looked more like a forest. Of course, this was supposed to be a *nice* view. Pretty trees and flowers and a pretty little fregging stream. It was so fregging blatant that he wondered how stupid the Authorities could be. Admittedly, he'd spent a lot of time staring at it while he was in his cell, but that was only because there was nothing else to do. The room was almost bare, with a bunk and a table and a side door to a small bathroom—and the big, unmovable door that led outside.

Of course, even Rats himself admitted it was in some ways better than where he used to live. But he'd still choose his old hole any day. It may have been stinky and loud and no bigger than this cell—but it was his. And he knew he wasn't going to walk out brainwashed to be a nice little fregging sheep when he went there.

Of course, Rats knew he could have been a better person. Nobody was perfect, and especially not in the slums. You couldn't afford it. But he *was* a good person, he knew that, as much as he could be. He stood up for his mates and helped people in need when he could afford to. He kept his word and his honor.

At one point, he'd even told it to them, when a couple of them were escorting him to one of their stupid, ineffective brainwashing sessions. He tried his best, he'd told them. The "crimes" they'd arrested him for, they had no idea what was really happening. Sure, he'd been violent, probably even killed someone—so what? They'd attacked first, and not just once. Of course, if you just came swooping to the scene in your fregging flying car at that moment, it would look like he was attacking, but it really wasn't like that. And if these guys were allowed to punish you for wrongdoing, why couldn't the people on the streets bust some heads too? Rats would never have hurt someone who didn't deserve it. And he lived down there, in the slums in the ruins—he knew what was going on and he had the right. *These* guys just came from somewhere outside and started kidnapping and brainwashing people.

Rats had seen what the victims became like, and they were too bad even for pity—he despised them. Like that tweet who ran the Charity Church. Of course, Rats had nothing against helping people, but he was such a fregging eunuch. Besides, he helped everyone equally, the zips and tooks as well as decent White people. Rats could even have understood staying outside the gangs and helping everyone regardless, but feeding the pests was only going to end up bad for everyone. Every time you helped a zip, you might as well be kicking a real person in the face.

But no, these high-and-mighty Authorities thought they knew everything better and made you love everyone equally. They'd never been ganged up on by the tooks or listen to yet another sobbing woman having been raped by the zips. They were "tolerant," which meant they only thought it was a crime if White people did it.

And the worst crime of all—wasn't that just what *they* were doing? Brainwashing good people to be like them? Truth be told, Rats feared nothing as much as it working on him. So far, it was having no effect at all, but he sensed vaguely that there was going to be more. And everyone knew it worked on almost anyone.

Everyone also knew that if it didn't, they'd just kill you. He was hoping they'd kill him.

Rats stared morosely out of the window. There were colorful birds in the trees. That almost cheered him up.

* * *

Some guards opened the door to bring in food. He'd tried fighting his way past them once, but it had been no use. He didn't even remember what happened other than that he'd been out cold almost immediately and woken up later with his meal neatly laid out and getting cold. The food was good, he had to admit, but he still ate grudgingly and left some over.

He took a nap, knowing that soon after lunch, it would be brainwashing time again. Sure enough, he was awoken by the sound of the door opening again.

"Hello," Jeremy said and stepped inside, flanked by a couple of guards. They also said hello, and one of them picked up his plate. Jeremy sounded friendly enough, and the two guards sounded business-like, but of course Rats wasn't fooled.

Jeremy was Rats' personal brainwasher. He was tall and stout and wore a mustache he could have done without, though Rats wasn't about to give him any fregging fashion tips. He must have been specifically trained to be pleasant; Rats sometimes found it hard to hate him, even knowing what he did. He even seemed a little sorry that they were doing this to Rats, although he'd also expressed a firm opinion that Rats had done wrong.

"You come to take me in for brainwashing?" Rats said sarcastically. He sensed that, carefully though Jeremy hid his feelings, calling it that was one thing that got to him.

Jeremy looked down at him inscrutably. "Actually, yes. Today we do what you would call the brainwashing."

It was an instinctive reaction. Rage and despair exploded Rats from where he was sitting on the bed and out toward his tormentors. He might have torn out Jeremy's throat.

But of course, he got nowhere. One of the guards pulled out some fancy techno weapon and pointed and clicked him into unconsciousness.

* * *

When Rats woke up, he found that he was tethered to a wheelchair. He also found that he was drugged somehow, because the thought of raging in despair died as soon as it was born. His head was fuzzy and there was an odd sense of pleasure. So, he had to contend himself with a quiet, nagging sense of despair.

"Aw, hell," he muttered, leaning his head back on a pillow. "I'm sorry about this."

Rats turned his head to the side and saw Jeremy, walking by him. And he saw that they were just about to walk past a door—room 3B, where all the previous brainwashing sessions had taken place.

So this was really it. It was going to be something different—the part where they broke you.

Idly, he wondered what all the other sessions had been about. He'd thought it had been ridiculous. They'd put this cap with all the wires on his head, and he'd been so furious and terrified they'd had to drug him like this at first, but then they'd done almost nothing. They'd just given him... history lessons. Things he didn't care about and barely paid attention to, though the device had forcibly input it in his brain and he'd noticed bits of it had stuck.

It was about the history of the City, and how the Authorities had come to be there. A lot of stuff about how it had once been a great, wealthy city where life had been much better, but then there had been a civil war and a collapse... And then the Authorities had come and they just had to do *something*. So they started a police force, and they started applying the dreaded Punishment. They didn't want to, but, the brain-movies said, they couldn't leave things as they were...

There had been more to it—whole three sessions of history—but this seemed to have been the point. And, as the drug's effect began to weaken, Rats realized something about this was starting to terrify him. Something that his brain had been working out on his own, while he wasn't looking, from all the stuff shoved into it. He could feel the dull terror before he was able to articulate the thought in his mind.

They really believed in it. They really believed they had to do this. They really wanted to help. That was why they were so fregging apologetic all the time; they even knew what they were doing was bad, but they thought they had to do it.

Thinking all this only took a few seconds. "It doesn't matter, you know," Rats heard himself saying.

"Pardon?"

Rats waved a hand, though it was a very small wave since his wrist was restrained. "Doesn't matter what you're all doing this for, Jeremy. It's still fregging brainwashing. It's just wrong. You can't do that to me, period. Doesn't matter what your reasons."

Jeremy sighed. "I know what you mean. But you're also wrong—it's not at all as bad as you think. And you do have a choice, in the end. And no, we won't kill you if you don't do as we want."

"Like freg you won't."

"Of course, I also know all of these are things real brainwashers would tell you beforehand. All I can say is, wait and see."

"Wait until I'm brainwashed and see?"

"I know, I know..."

"Because I can't make a choice after that, can I? You've... already made it for me."

"I know. It's not really... but there's no point in talking about this. And even though it's not like you imagine, we still think it might be a bad thing, because it's still too much like brainwashing. But we've also seen the alternative. And really, in some ways it's a lot like if you were simply educated the right way when you were little..."

Rats laughed hollowly. His head was starting to clear, although there was liable to be a migraine. Still, he didn't feel like fighting now.

"I hope I'll die. I'd rather. And in a sense, maybe I will, anyway, if there's nothing left but your zombie slave."

Jeremy didn't reply. Instead, he opened a door: Room A1. "We're here."

* * *

Rats was past despair and fear. He didn't struggle. This was going to be the end for him anyway; all he wanted to do now was to guilt Jeremy, to somehow show him that he was wrong and Rats was right. To somehow show this nice man that he was killing him.

The thought that Jeremy was killing him out of kindness was almost scarier than the same thought about the Authorities, because Jeremy had a face, was a man. Rats found himself for the first time less afraid of what would happen to him and more spiritually terrified at the state of humankind. Atrocities done for good intentions; how did you cope with that? They were walking around doing evil things and they thought they were good. He'd met hypocrites and idiots before, of course, but this was all so... so *philosophical*.

As in Room 3B, there was a chair with restraints in front of a monitor, with ominous technothingies hanging over it and on its sides. Rats let himself be attached without opposition, with only a shiver.

The complicated plastic harness on his head was even more complicated this time. It took minutes for Jeremy and some others to put it on. Finally, they told him to relax. A big text saying "TESTING" solidified slowly into his view. It wasn't on the monitor but seemingly hovering in the air and moving with his eyes. This, too, was familiar.

"Need some adjustments at 36 and 42," someone said out of sight. Someone fiddled with the probes atop his skull. TESTING came up again, looking just the same in his opinion, but this time they deemed everything to be working all right.

At least the clamps on his head were comfortable. He could even move his neck a little and lean on a kind of pillow. It would still get uncomfortable, he knew this from experience, but only after several minutes.

Then he began to see auras and his head swam. He could feel his hair standing up from the electricity. It was beginning.

* * *

Rats blacked out very briefly, and when he came back to, his mind was floating in a fuzzy imaginary space that mostly concealed the reality around him. He remembered where he was but couldn't really see or feel or hear it. Nor smell. Instead, a familiar smell rose up; something mildly unpleasant but familiar, a smell whose origin he didn't know and that he had barely noticed before. A smell from his home streets.

It felt almost as if he was there again. They were raising up his memories, or feeding him a new version of them—who knew. He had a vague sense at first of just being there, superficially skipping through all kinds of familiar scenarios. Then the show began.

He saw himself doing things—and soon he realized these

were the crimes he was being accused of—and not too long after that, he began laughing in the real world, hollow, a little manic, a sound that pushed its way even into this induced dream. Because he had won; they weren't going to brainwash him after all.

He saw himself mugging someone; in a gang fight; pushing around some zip kids; stealing from a shop. He even saw the one that had got him arrested and that had secretly been troubling him—a violent scuffle where he'd stabbed more than one person, starting from another gang dispute.

But he also saw that he had been right, all along. He'd had no choice; or, it hadn't been that bad, after all; or, they totally had it coming; or, he was just standing up for his buddies. Usually it was about all of these each time. He remembered now why he'd done those things, and he didn't regret them at all. Even the last big fight—they'd had it coming, and he was only standing up for himself, and they would have done worse.

These fregging idiots had thought they could make him cower in front of them by showing how bad he was—but in the cold light of the facts, he didn't regret anything.

The images died out, and the real world began to swim back into focus. Rats struggled to gain control of his mouth to say something. But instead, he heard Jeremy's voice next to his ear.

"That was the first part—how it felt like to you."

Then the virtual reality snapped back on, and Rats was seeing something different.

He was an awkward, fat man, walking in the street, looking around nervously, sweating uncomfortably. He'd only come to this part of town because he was running out of money and there was a job, but he was scared...

He was a member of a gang, and it was so familiar he thought it was his own, until he realized it was the other one...

He was a kid, walking around and joking with some other kids—they forgot to be afraid because they were zips for a while...

He was a shopkeeper, struggling to make ends meet, constantly afraid of thieves because they were everywhere, but really, if they only stole from him, he would be lucky they hadn't hurt him...

And then *he was scared to death when this big thug stepped in front of him. And he took all his money and he would go hungry that week, but that wasn't enough, the leering thug pushed him around and almost made him wet his pants, and he went away fighting tears of rage.*

...The gangs got into a fight, and the one he was in now was clearly in the right, but those other bastards went pushing way past their rights and hurt some of his mates. And one of them was Rats.

...A couple of big, mean white bullies started shouting at them, and they called them names and said a lot of nasty things they didn't even understand properly, and they were afraid they would die if they didn't play nice, and the bullies hit them and pushed them to the ground and it hurt.

...He was counting out his money and it was not enough, it was never enough, and he cursed the fregging thieves who seemed to have taken as much stuff as he had managed to sell.

He was in the other gang again, and they got into mouthing off with the enemy, and those bastards went way too far, and when the fight began, one of them pulled out a knife, totally out of nowhere, and he was stabbed, and the pain was horrible, and he fell down to the ground and knew he was going to die...

* * *

Rats actually blacked out again when he died in his dream. When he snapped back into reality, he screamed hoarsely.

This hadn't been just images or information, it had been emotions, it had been perspectives, it had been *being* the other person. Yet, he wasn't. He was Rats. And he was a monster, a leering, terrifying bully, a vicious thug from the other gang, a faceless, heartless thief, the face of death and pain at the other end of the dagger. You saw other people that way all the time, but never yourself. You *couldn't* see yourself like that. All the defense mechanisms had been stripped away, all that the ego normally relied on, and the contempt, hatred, fear and above all pain of others struck at him like knives to the soul.

He was twisting and struggling in his chair—he realized as he came back to reality—and shouting something. It might have been *"Kill me!"*

If he had felt such things toward someone else, he *would* have killed them.

A needle injected another dose of calming drug into his arm. He twitched a few last times and then just stayed there, panting. He was physically calmed down, but the drug didn't really make the pain go away. He still felt numbly horrible.

"I'm sorry, Rats," Jeremy said by his ear. "It will get better. That was the second part: how it felt to the others. Now comes the third part—the multiplex view."

The virtual reality engulfed him again.

* * *

Rats calmed down, as if by command, which it obviously was. He now had a sense of surveying the whole city as if floating above it, and also along the streets. And then he started seeing the same events again, from a point of view he couldn't have imagined. It was as if he were everyone and no one; several people at once but beyond any of them. And both taking part and an outsider.

There were both of the gangs, both really about the same, but both hating each other's guts because of old events—events, he saw, that had a lot to do with everyone looking out for their own group and being unfair toward the other. Any time either gang took revenge, the other thought they'd gone too far; and then they'd take revenge again, and the others would think they were starting it all over again when the score had just been settled.

There was the mugged fat man, but there was also the mugger, himself. The mugger thought he needed the money more badly and it served the guy right for coming to the wrong part of town, but he wouldn't have thought so if he knew how the fat man felt and how *he* needed the money. And even if he had really needed the money more, he shouldn't have gone on a power trip and frightened the guy so much. But the fat man was also wrong, because he feared and hated the mugger and saw him as only a monster who was doing it almost for fun. It had been wrong to rob him, Rats realized, but he also saw why he hadn't seen this before. He had been stupid and selfish, and he had been bad, but he had never meant to be *that* bad.

There were the zip kids, who'd done nothing bad and just wanted to goof around with their friends and barely even understood about this whole race thing, except they were already starting to learn they needed to be afraid, and ashamed of who they were, and that wasn't right. And there was Rats and the other guy who had pushed them around, and *they* had been taught to despise and hate zips, and even when they looked at a couple of kids, they didn't even see them as real kids. They were very wrong, but they didn't see it; again, they were not really monsters, just stupid and blind to the unfairness of their own thinking. They would have never knowingly been so unfair. In a blinding flash of double feeling, Rats was himself pushing the kid down and the kid at the same time, and he understood himself as he had never before. He was hurting a kid of less than ten years old, but all he saw at the moment was... this annoying object that he hated and wanted to be rid of somehow. He'd balked after that, seeing he was going too far, but it was nothing compared to the kid's terror and emotional hurt, worse than the physical pain.

And there was the merchant struggling for money and counting every penny and feeling hurt and exposed when he was stolen from, but there was also the thief who was also struggling for money. At that point, Rats felt less guilty about stealing than about stupidly thinking he wasn't hurting anyone. At the very least, even though he had a real need, he should have taken less. Probably not even that.

Finally, there was the fight where he may have killed people. And he saw a couple of gangs, mirror images of each other, trading insults, escalating it because they were itching to fight. What struck him was that they had really thought that pent-up anger and defending your honor against mere words had been worth it, had justified it—this fight where people had been hurt and even, perhaps, killed.

Rats' mind was flooded with new thoughts, feelings, understandings. He could barely think straight, but he knew he had a lot to think about. Had he known of it, he would have been grateful of being made to drift into peaceful, normal sleep afterwards.

* * *

Rats awoke feeling strangely light and empty. He wasn't sure, but he may actually have been feeling good. He sensed through his eyelids that morning light was flooding through the window in his cell.

"Good morning, Rats. How are you feeling now?"

Rats opened his eyes and saw Jeremy sitting on a chair by his bed in the cell. He was smiling, but looking at him with some concern. A surge of emotions flashed through Rats' mind, starting with the negative but settling down to something surprisingly positive. He realized how much he would have liked Jeremy if he hadn't had such strong reasons not to. The man had a quiet kind of strength, different from what he was used to on the streets but very real.

And as for those reasons...

"That... was that the brainwashing?"

"Yes. All of it," Jeremy said. "And now I can tell you something else too, that you couldn't have understood before."

"What's that?"

"I've been through that as well. Most of us here have."

"You used to be criminals?"

"Some of us, but that's not what I meant. We wanted to make sure we were doing the right thing in the end."

"I'm not sure what..."

"We made ourselves see this 'brainwashing' from the point of view of the subjects as well. I've seen what it feels like, both before and after, the way you felt how you had hurt people. Of course, we can't *prove* it's right that way, because we need to have the multiplex debriefing for our sanity, and we need to take an active hand in designing what it shows. But let me tell you, it was a real eye-opener. That's why we're so sorry we need to make you do something like this against your will."

"But I get to make a free choice what to do now? Is that what you've been getting at?"

"Yes. Everyone's free to go after this, because they've had their punishment and so few people go back to committing crimes as they used to. Of course, if they do, we may have to arrest them again and prescribe old-fashioned jail time or counseling. Fortunately, that really is rare."

"Yeah, that was punishment all right..."

"Personally, I think it's the one right punishment for anyone. Just to *see* the harm... although we can't leave it at that or it might break people for good. I... hope you feel you've recovered by now and understand more? And why we're doing this?"

"Yeah... I guess I do, though I have a lot of thinking to do. Before I decide anything, too."

"Of course. And a lot of people want to study after this, too."

"Study?"

"Psychology and sociology and evolutionary psychology and things like that. To put words to what they've been directly shown. You could never understand these things so well from just reading books... I mean, it's the kind of thing you can tell people and often they'll nod, yes, of course, I understand that, and then they go right back to thinking like they did before. But anyway, once you have understood them like this, the theory can help you put it all together."

"Books?"

"Also, videos and interactive computer programs, if you prefer. Also, novels and movies if you want to explore it through art."

"Yeah, I might... look at some of those."

"You can do as you wish. This was the last time you had to stay in this cell. You can move to the open ward now. There will also be others like you who you can talk to."

* * *

When Rats made his decision after several surprisingly pleasant days, he realized it had been at the back of his head from the start. He asked if he could go and help at the Charity Church. He could. And so he worked there, patiently, day to day, helping the helpless and enduring the threats and taunts of people like he used to be. He had to keep reminding himself of why they were that way, but he never did forget, and so he was always patient. He even got through to some of them and converted them to work with him. Little by very little, they made the City a better place to live for everyone.

He never did figure out whether it was really brainwashing or not.

* * *

This story first appeared in the After Dinner Conversation—July 2022 issue.

Discussion Questions

1. Do you think what they did to Rats was brainwashing? What is your working definition of brainwashing and how does it apply, or not apply, to what happened to Rats?
2. If this treatment really existed, do you think it would work? What % of the time do you think it would work?
3. Is there really a difference between understanding how your actions affect others, and actually living the interactions from their perspective? What, if anything, is the difference, and why does it exist?
4. Traditional prisons hold your body, but you maintain your free will within its confines. Is forcing someone to live an experience without free will an acceptable form of punishment?
5. If a punishment like the one in the story were possible, would you support its implementation? What levels of crimes would it be acceptable for, and what level would be too low to warrant its use?

* * *

Human Contact

Frances Howard-Snyder

* * *

Beer tasted like wet money—or maybe just bad beer did. Viola had never tried any other kind. She preferred white wine, but there was no white wine at this party.

"Drink it like medicine," the guy manning the keg said. "It'll loosen you up." He wore a peacoat, a fedora, and dark-rimmed glasses. Said his name was Greg.

When some of the beer spilled on her chin, Viola swiped at it with the sleeve of her zippered hoody and burped. Greg refilled her cup. Feeling a little dizzy, she took a handful of potato chips and marveled at the miracle of salt and grease.

"You're a student, yeah?" he said, drawing a pipe from his pocket. "What classes are you taking?"

"History 103, Greek, and Philosophy 207."

"Who'd you have for philosophy?" He fiddled with lighting up the pipe. Viola guessed he was a graduate student.

"Wilson. She's very cool. We're learning about testimonial injustice."

"Oh yeah."

Viola couldn't tell whether this meant he knew what testimonial injustice was or whether he was asking for an explanation. She plowed ahead anyway. "Some people's views are taken less seriously than others'. They don't get respected as knowers or sources of knowledge. Their testimony is discounted."

"Let me guess. Those people are usually..." He mimed *thinking hard*. "Could they be... women?"

Viola took another swig from the clear plastic cup, squeezing it tight enough to crack it. "Yes, among others."

"How astonishing," he said, blew a couple of smoke rings, filled his own glass, and then offered to refill her cup.

"I think it is," she said. "Where'd you get the glass?"

He pointed at the yellow cupboard over the coffee maker before moving outside. The glass she found had a half-faded decal of a four-leaf clover but was heavy and firm, classier than the broken plastic cup. She filled it, took a long medicinal swig and decided to go outside herself. The little back courtyard smelled of smoke and something sweet, maybe cooking pumpkin. As her eyes got used to the lower light, she made out a wall covered with a creeping plant, a string of Christmas lights, a broken grill, some planters, and half a dozen people in a loose circle. Viola pulled her jacket tight around her and wished she hadn't obeyed the posted instructions to remove her shoes at the front door.

She recognized one of the voices from the circle: a sophomore from Viola's dorm, one of the cool kids, someone she would like to have been friends with. She considered walking over and starting a conversation. But then a blonde girl with a streak of purple in her hair offered her a joint.

Viola had never smoked a joint before, but why not? Everyone said it was harmless, a lot safer than alcohol, and legal, at least if you were twenty-one. She was only eighteen, but that hadn't kept her from the beer. She gripped the small, damp object between her thumb and forefinger and felt a moment of fear—like when the dentist starts the drill. Would she be able to handle this? She put her lips to the saliva-moistened tip and inhaled deeply, drawing the smoke into her mouth and lungs.

"Hold it for a few seconds," the girl said.

She obeyed until she had to cough.

A few people laughed languidly. "First time?"

"That obvious?" Viola laughed with them, hoping they were laughing with her.

The joint came around again. The first hit hadn't had much effect aside from the coughing fit. Determined to do better this time, she took a smaller hit.

"What do you think?" a man beside her asked. About six-foot tall, with a bulky body, he had jutting ears, round glasses and a receding hairline.

"I'm not feeling much, I'm afraid. Except cold."

"Come sit down." He took off his jacket in a wide, expansive motion, folded it and set it on the edge of a planter that contained shriveled tomato plants.

She sat. "Thank you. Oh, but this is silly. You'll be cold."

"I'm fine. I'm warm-blooded." He flexed his biceps under the tight t-shirt. "Philip." He held out a large hand.

"Viola."

"That's an interesting name."

"My mother named me after her favorite Shakespearean

character."

"Did you come to the party with anyone?"

"Not exactly. This guy in my history study group told me about it. I thought it might be fun. I've been working every night for two weeks. I needed a break."

He scrutinized her face. "What are you looking for, Viola?"

This was one of those deep questions people asked when they were stoned. Answers like "the bathroom" or "more potato chips" wouldn't do. Did she have an adequate answer? Would she give it to a stranger if she did? A moat of reserve surrounded her most of the time—to keep her safe, to keep her secrets close, to protect herself. But what if she wanted to share her secrets? What if what she really wanted was that skin-to-skin connection where there were no barriers, no deception, nothing withheld, where she was no longer alone? She shuffled through her deck of desires. *To be special? To be seen as special?* "Human contact," she finally said with a small laugh, half-hoping he would hear her as ironic, and half-hoping he wouldn't.

He smiled, but she couldn't tell what he'd heard. "Where do you live?"

"Higgenson Hall."

"Ah, dorm life!"

Living in a dorm was something to be a little embarrassed about, she sensed. "I'm moving out next fall."

"Don't do that. Dorms are cool. Hang on as long as you can. Everything's taken care of for you. Food, cleaning, no worries about commuting or parking."

"Yeah. Like when you're a kid. My mom calls it adulting with training wheels."

He laughed. "Is that supposed to be a good thing or a bad thing?"

"A good thing, I think. She wants me to be safe. I had a pretty sheltered childhood."

He nodded, and Viola realized this must be obvious.

"Would you like me to walk you home?" he asked. "I'm leaving now. I have to write an essay."

Viola looked into his face trying to discern his intentions. Was his offer dangerous? Might he try to kiss her or seduce her or worse? Or was it the safe option—an escort across the two streets off campus and then across campus itself, depositing her safely at the front door of her dorm at 10:30. He looked safe. But she didn't want safe. "No," she said finally. "I don't have a paper to write or a test in the morning. I think I'll stay out until midnight."

He shrugged and said, "Suit yourself," as if he were disappointed. Because he wanted a kiss or because he wanted to keep her safe, she couldn't tell.

She felt bad about disappointing him either way. "Maybe I'll see you around. Good luck with your essay." She stood, brushed off his jacket, and handed it back to him.

He bent and kissed her cheek. "Take care of yourself."

As he clanged through the screen door, Viola wondered whether she'd made a mistake. She imagined Philip's big hands caressing her and felt an ache between her legs. She hadn't had sex since the first weekend of October, when she'd been home and reunited with her high school boyfriend, Steve. That was before he suggested that it made sense for them to start seeing other people, and she'd told him to go screw himself. She missed it, in spite of the mess and complications. Whoa! Viola. Where were these thoughts coming from? Did pot give you the munchies for sex as well as for potato chips?

The smokers were heading back inside. Viola drained her glass and followed. Back in the kitchen, she blinked in the brighter light and looked around for someone to talk to. She poured herself another glass of the lukewarm beer and moved towards where Greg was talking to two women, who looked like grad students.

"I'm pissed as heck about all this adulation Kobe Bryant is getting. He was a rapist. We can't forget that," the shorter, red-haired woman said.

"Did you hear about how Gayle King got death threats just for asking a question about Kobe's rape case in an interview?" a tall woman with broad shoulders added.

"He was a real hero to a lot a people," Greg said.

"Well, he shouldn't have been," the redhead said.

"I heard a comedian claim the real hero was the pilot who forgot to gas up his chopper. The guy got fired," Greg said. "I'd fire him too."

The small woman wheeled on him, "I don't care how many three-point shots you make or how many blocks or assists you get, a rapist is a rapist. And hundreds of millions of dollars in earnings and a helicopter crash doesn't change that fact."

Her voice rose and she slammed her fist down on the counter.

"The charges were dropped, and he denied it," Greg said softly, blowing another smoke ring. "Come on! Think of his wife and kids."

The woman drew in breath to speak.

Into the brief lull, Viola said. "Like my mom always says,

'Even pricks turn into top blokes after death!'"

She thought that might get a laugh.

It didn't. The redheaded woman looked her up and down for a long moment and then shifted her shoulders, so she was angled away from her and responded to Greg. "Well, I, for one, am not in mourning."

Viola took another deep swig. Needing to refill her empty glass, she moved back a few steps. Members of the group adjusted their positions so that their backs were towards her. Oh well. They didn't seem like very nice people anyway. She put her hand into the potato chip bowl and found only salt and crumbs. She hadn't had any dinner. Perhaps there'd be something to eat in the fridge but no, only pickles, mayonnaise, out-of-date half and half, peanut butter. She considered eating a few tablespoons of peanut butter, but that would be socially unacceptable. Instead she topped up her glass and moved off in search of real food.

The lights were lower in the living room. The chip bowls were empty. Sam Smith's "Stay with Me" was playing on the stereo. One of her favorites. A few people were dancing lazily on the bare wood floor. She swayed in time to the music.

"Hello, Viola," a boy about her own age from one of her classes, said. "I'm glad you came." Was he the one who'd invited her? She struggled to retrieve his name—Bill, Tim, Todd?—but gave up.

"Hello," she said, more eagerly than she would have at another time.

"Like to dance?" He shuffled in a dance-like motion and held up a cup. He'd been less confident before. Alcohol made conversation easier; maybe it would make dancing easier too.

She felt the music moving through her. "OK, but I'm not a very good dancer."

He laughed and gestured towards the other shuffling figures. "Well, then you'll fit right in." He was funny. She liked that in a guy. He had a jutting Adam's apple and a halo of rusty, frizzy hair, but she wasn't perfect herself: short, not exactly svelte, with coarse black eyebrows. ("Some people pluck their eyebrows, you know," Steve had said after she told him to go screw himself.) You shouldn't be too picky about people. Love should be free and abundant, given to everyone who asked. She'd read that somewhere, she couldn't remember where. She'd been skeptical at first, suspecting that men said this sort of thing just to get laid, but now it seemed profound. She felt a whoosh of affection for the funny, plain boy beside her and for the whole world. She raised her arms up in a long oval. He stepped closer, put his arms around her waist and pulled her close. They moved together. When Sam Smith ended, and Florence and the Machine started, she looked up at him questioningly.

"Let's keep going." He smiled. "I think you're a fabulous dancer."

"That's only because you're drunk."

"Do you think *I'm* a fabulous dancer?" he asked.

"Maybe if I had another beer I would. Could you get me one?" She leaned against the wall while she waited.

Two of the dancers, who turned out to be Emilia and Katie from her dorm, came over and greeted her. "You doing all right?" Emilia asked. Lean, muscled, caramel brown with quarter-inch hair, Emilia was smart and outspoken, someone Viola would have liked to be friends with.

"Fantastic!" Viola said.

"We're going back. You want to come?"

Viola thought about it for a few seconds and then shook her head. The two girls moved away. She thanked the boy when he brought back her glass and took a drink. "Ah. Now I see how fabulous you are." She let the glass slip from her hand and heard some tinkling glass. Then she swayed back and forth, and side to side, in what she hoped was an alluring manner.

"Mmm. I like the way you move," he whispered into her hair.

She moved more, lifting her feet. When she dropped the left one the second time, she thought a scorpion had stung her. "Ow," she said, grabbing her foot. "What was that?"

He fell to his knees. "Silly Viola. You've broken a glass and cut your foot. Let me help you."

He put his arm around her and held her up while she hopped towards the bathroom, the not entirely sanitary bathroom, with toothpaste spatters across the mirror, yellow around the base of the toilet, and rust stains on the porcelain under the faucet. She sat on the edge of the tub while he ran the water, and gently lifted her foot. He held it under the stream of warm water until the bleeding stopped and then dried the wound with a wad of toilet paper. Tender. She tried to stand and felt a wave of dizziness. How much blood had she lost? She leaned against him. "Thank you."

He bent and kissed her mouth, a brief, moist clinking of teeth. "I hate to see you hurt."

She slid her hand under his t-shirt, feeling his smooth belly and slightly puffy chest, finding the softness endearingly vulnerable.

"Can you walk?"

"Don't need to walk." She leaned back so far he had to grab her.

Someone rattled the door.

"They'll be needing the bathroom. Let's find somewhere more private." He opened the door. "Sorry, man," he said to the person waiting outside. "Medical emergency." He puffed out a string of high-pitched giggles. The guy gave him a funny look and pushed past him into the bathroom.

Then Viola and he stumbled down the hall and into a bedroom that smelled of wet dog and old food. Just enough moonlight showed them where the bed was. His bedroom? She had no idea. If it was his bedroom, perhaps she could find a textbook or a wallet with his name in it. Or maybe not. She was exhausted. It was too dark to search now, and names didn't really matter anyway.

She fell back onto the mattress, far lower than she'd expected. "Help! I've fallen and I can't get up." She giggled.

He plopped down beside her. "I'll rescue you," he murmured and started kissing her neck, his bristles tickling her skin. She put her arms around him and drew him tight against her. His hand was under her t-shirt, scrabbling with her bra. She tried to undo his zipper. They giggled at their clumsy desperation and worked on their own clothes. He moved on top of her, with his pants around his ankles She pulled off her panties and then he was inside her, the sensation weird but oddly familiar. She laughed.

"What's so funny?"

"We fit together like a couple of Lego pieces. It's just sho fucking weird that adults do this—schmoosh their body partsh together like this."

"I don't think iz weird at all. I think iz the most natural thing in the world." He murmured in a slurred voice.

"No. It is really, really weird in our modern, civilized soshiety." She was probably slurring her words too. Her thoughts were certainly sloshing around haphazardly.

"Hush now," he murmured against her neck. "Stop talking. I need to concentrate."

The room lurched over her, alternating moonlight and dark, back and forth like a boat on choppy water. She hoped the motion wouldn't make her sick. He breathed faster and louder and gave a brief grunt of ecstasy. She moved under him, wondering when her own ecstasy would happen but found herself nodding off and bumping awake. At some point, they both must have fallen asleep.

A spear of light pricked her awake. A powerful flashlight? No, more like sunlight breaking through a gap in the makeshift curtains. Where was she? The room had bookshelves made of concrete blocks and planks, clothes everywhere, and a bare bulb hanging from the ceiling. The mattress she lay on was directly on the floor. Not her dorm room.

Her mouth tasted like a cracked ashtray that someone had thrown up in; her head hurt; she needed to pee, but she couldn't find the energy to push herself up off the low mattress. Eventually the pressure in her bladder made her stand. Only then did she notice the unconscious man on the other side of the bed, his pants around his ankles, revealing pale buttocks. His arm was raised up beside his rusty, frizzy head. The guy from her history class. What was his name? What had happened between them? Realizing she was half-naked too, she touched her pubic hair. Sticky. Ew! No. God no! She hadn't. What could she have been thinking? She had to get away.

She stood, trying not to make a noise or shift the mattress, pulled on her panties, grabbed her purse, and tiptoed to the door. Her foot hurt, but she was in too much of a hurry to care. A sound from the bed made her look around. Just a small, plaintive fart. Her bedmate was still asleep. She turned the handle and gently pulled, then slipped out and drew the door closed without letting it click.

In the bathroom, she peed but didn't flush, and examined the cut on her foot. Unable to remember how she'd hurt it, she scraped off most of the bloody toilet paper. Then she padded down the hall, retrieved her shoes, and headed out onto the dark red, concrete porch and into the sunlit street. She shivered at the chilly breeze that pierced the warmth and wished she'd brought sunglasses. She'd forgotten her hoody, but she was not going back for it. No way. She'd escaped. Nobody need ever know what she'd done. Her head throbbed, a good reminder never to drink that much again.

Three people were lounging in the common area on her floor. Maya, the dorm RA, leaned back on the scruffy yellow and orange sofa in lavender silk pajamas. Lizzy, a slight girl with thin blond hair, was kneeling on the rug in front of the coffee table in a long flannel nightshirt, making waffles and pouring juice into cups on the coffee table.

Emilia in short cotton PJ's was leaning against the foosball table. "Yo, Viola," she called, "Where've you been?"

"Just out for a walk. Isn't this weather lovely?" Rare February sunlight tumbled down through the dust and Viola wished again that she had her sunglasses.

Emilia grinned cheerfully. "In the same clothes you wore last night, smelling of beer and cum? A likely story."

Viola's cheeks heated fast. She considered running down the hallway to her room but that would look idiotic. Better to brazen it out. "Give me a glass of juice."

"Waffles?" Lizzy asked. "Are you all right?"

"Just a little queasy. I think waffles might make me throw up. But I'm really thirsty and OJ will get the icky taste out of my mouth."

"Who was he?" Emilia asked, handing her a cup.

The reconstituted juice was too thick, too sweet, and too sour. Viola screwed up her mouth. "Just a guy from my history class."

"Name?"

Emilia had such a strong personality you couldn't tell her to mind her own business. "I didn't catch his name." Viola laughed, hoping to sound casual and brash.

Emilia's agile face broke into another grin. "God, you're a slut!"

Maya, the oldest of the three, and the dorm RA, frowned.

"Yeah, but we've all been there." Viola glanced around the circle. "You've done stupid things like this, right?"

Lizzy shivered. "No way."

Emilia shrugged. "I prefer girls. And I prefer to know their names. I have standards."

Maya shook her head, her long black hair swinging like two funeral sheets. "I came close once. But my friends kept me safe."

"Safe?" Viola closed her eyes and pressed her thumbs into her pounding temples.

"What's wrong, Viola?" Lizzy came and put an arm around her. "Did he hurt you?"

"It's just a hangover." Viola picked up a waffle and started ripping it into pieces.

Maya asked, "How much did you drink?"

Underage drinking was illegal. Maya was some sort of quasi-authority figure here. Would she report her? Could Viola be kicked out of school or even arrested? She shouldn't have mentioned the alcohol. "I'm in trouble, aren't I?" She chewed on a mouthful of waffle that tasted like damp cardboard, and then took another bite. She felt hungry and full at the same time.

Maya patted her arm and spoke in a low, urgent voice. "No, silly. You're not in trouble. I'm in your corner—always. It's my job to protect you. But this is important. Just think, how many drinks did you have?"

Viola closed her eyes and tried to remember. She'd had two drinks in the plastic cup in the kitchen, and then a third in the glass. Had she poured a fourth? It was hard to remember. There had been a lot of topping up of half-full glasses. Then she'd gone outside and returned and poured another and then when she'd been shut out of that conversation about Kobe Bryant, she'd poured herself more, and then History Guy had brought her another glass. "Seven," she said slowly and uncertainly. "Or maybe six or eight." *Don't mention the pot*, she told herself.

"And were you eating?"

"Just a few potato chips."

"God, Viola, you're a fool," Emilia said. "If I'd realized, I'd have come and kicked your ass."

Maya glared at her. "No, victim-blaming, Emilia. I will not

tolerate that. You know better."

Lizzy gasped. "Oh, Viola. I feel so bad for you."

"Did he wear a condom, Viola?" Maya asked.

Viola tried to remember. Long paragraphs of the night before were redacted, just black patches. "I don't remember," she muttered.

"Really? God, you were messed up."

"You know what this means, don't you?" Lizzy said.

"That I'd better go see if I can get a morning-after pill?" Viola groaned inwardly. She didn't need any more hassle. All she wanted was to sleep for eighteen hours.

"Well, yes. Absolutely. But also, if you were that drunk, you couldn't consent. Sex without consent is rape. We had a lecture about that during Orientation. Don't you remember? They made it very clear." Lizzy pointed towards a poster on the wall that read, *Sexual Violence Awareness Day*. Someone had crossed out "day" and replaced it with "CENTURY". Then she pulled out her laptop and typed fast. Eventually she found the page she was looking for and turned the screen so Viola could see it. The page confirmed what she'd said.

Viola tried to laugh. "I'll get over it. I just need a long shower, some Alka-Seltzer, and a nap, and I'll be fine."

"Don't shower," Maya said gently. "Let's figure this out first. We may need to take you to the hospital..."

"Who was this guy, Viola?" Emilia asked again.

"I told you. I didn't catch his name."

"But was he someone you liked? Someone you were attracted to?"

Viola tried to picture his face but drew a blank. She burped and the acid taste reminded her of his moon-pale buttocks and Adam's apple. "God no! Not in a million years. Not if I'd been in my right mind."

Maya tsked softly. "Not a good sign. Sounds like the alcohol made all the difference. Lizzy is right. If you're not in your right mind, as you put it, you can't legally consent."

Viola remembered the two of them stumbling down the hallway and banging into the thin walls. She remembered his clumsy fingers fiddling ineptly with her bra, remembered his slurred words. "But he was drunk too."

"Drunkenness is no excuse for rape," Lizzy said.

"That's ridiculous," Emilia said. "If they were both drunk, he might as well claim Viola raped him." She rolled her eyes so hard you'd had to worry they'd get trapped behind her brain.

"That's stupid. Women can't rape men," Lizzy said.

"Why not?"

Lizzy and Emilia glared at each other. Viola's stomach gurgled.

"Calm down, guys," Maya said. "Yelling won't help. Viola doesn't need any extra stress. The rule, as I understand it..." She took the computer and did some Googling. "Is that in those situations, it's the person who makes the first move who can be charged with assault."

"Well?" Lizzy asked Viola. "Who made the first move?"

Viola covered her face with her hands and tried to remember. "He asked me to dance." She flashed to the scene in the bathroom. "I leaned against him. He kissed me."

"Did he ask your permission before he kissed you?" Lizzy asked.

"We weren't talking much."

Lizzy's jaw tightened. She'd made up her mind.

Emilia was shaking her head.

Viola looked at Maya, expecting her to cast the deciding vote.

But Maya put a hand out to shush Lizzy and turned to Viola. "It's up to you, Sweetheart. As a wise psychologist once said to me, 'You know when you're assaulted. If you feel assaulted, you were assaulted.'"

Viola leaned back and thought about how she felt. Had she been a silly little fool or had she been assaulted? Should she take a shower, give herself a mental kick in the pants, or should she be rushed to the hospital, and then to the Title IX office and then perhaps to the police station?

She replayed the rollercoaster ride she'd taken on the mattress on the floor of the strange bedroom. "It didn't feel *that* bad last night."

"You sometimes see things more clearly in retrospect," Lizzy said. "My cousin got seduced by her gym teacher when she was in high school. She told me she loved him at the time, and then she felt guilty. It took a couple of years for her to realize that he'd violated her."

Viola's eyes widened as she tried to take this in. "I don't know," she whispered, Maya's formula seemed so simple, but Viola didn't know how she felt. She felt *terrible*—screaming head, pounding pulse, sour stomach, jittery—but was that the right kind of terrible? She thought of all the terrible things, that disgusting beer, the arrogant grad student Greg, and those pissy women who wouldn't laugh at her joke and made her feel like dirt and the nerdy boy who took advantage of her drunkenness and oh shit! She stood and ran from the room, just making it to the bathroom in time. The beer tasted like anti-freeze coming up. She flushed, moved to the sink, and then splashed some water on her face and found her toothbrush.

She gazed at her stupid eyebrows in the mirror. Maybe Steve was right. Maybe she should pluck them or shave them or whatever people do with eyebrows.

She didn't want everyone to know about what happened. What would her parents say?

Her mother was going to call for their weekly facetime convo at 11. Maybe Viola should ask her. Her mother had more experience; she'd know what Viola should do. But she—Viola could just tell—would say that Viola had been a damned fool for getting drunk and getting herself into this absurd situation. *Viola should just quit this binge drinking and take better care of herself because if she didn't, she'd just be wasting all the hard-earned money her parents had put into Viola's college account and she might as well drop out and get a job at Fred Meyer's.* According to her mother's definition, Viola had not been assaulted. But her mother's definition—she'd learned at the Orientation—was outdated. By the new, updated version, maybe she had been. Who was to say?

She'd have to decide. But just not yet. First, she needed to puke up more of that wet-money beer.

* * *

This story first appeared in the After Dinner Conversation—August 2020 issue.

Discussion Questions

1. Was Viola raped by the boy she had sex with? What are the deciding (*and irrelevant*) factors in your assessment? Can there ever be consent when one (*or both*) of the partners are intoxicated? Does it matter that Viola never said stop, and that she expressed (*albeit drunken*) interest in having sex with the boy? Can the boy assert he was raped because kissing Viola does not mean he consented to have sex with her?

2. What do you believe are the appropriate criminal punishments? If you believe he/she should go to prison, how long should he/she go to prison for?

3. Is the owner (*or renter*) of the property in any way responsible for providing alcohol to Viola and others who were not of legal drinking age? Are they responsible for the potential criminality of the sexual encounter?

4. Assuming Viola believes she was raped, should there be a statute of limitations to bring criminal charges? Do you think it would be ethical for Viola to reveal she was raped decades later to keep the boy from being appointed to a high-profile position? What if she does not assert it was rape, but only her memory and *others* call it rape?

5. In the story, Maya says, "You know when you're assaulted. If you *feel* assaulted, you were assaulted." Do you agree with this statement? Does it matter that Viola didn't *feel* assaulted until talking to her friends?

* * *

Author Information

Idle Horns

Garrett Davis is a plumber by day and writer whenever he can muster the courage. He lives in B.C.

Community of Peers

Dean Gessie's short stories and poetry have appeared in numerous anthologies around the world and he has won multiple international prizes. He has also published three novellas with Anaphora Literary Press: Guantanamo Redux; A Brief History of Summer Employment; and TrumpeterVille.

Form Seven Alpha

Richard Pettigrew is Professor of Philosophy at the University of Bristol in the UK. He started writing philosophical fiction in 2021. In his philosophical research, he asks how we should reason well about the world while being uncertain what it's like. In his fiction writing, he likes to explore questions about what we value and why, and how we should treat ourselves and others. X (Twitter) *@Wiglet1981*; *www.richardpettigrew.com*

Conscience Cleaners

Alexander B. Joy lives and works in his native New Hampshire, where he spends the long winters reading the world's classics and composing haiku. In the nonfiction realm, he typically writes about literature, film, and philosophy. X (Twitter) *@aeneas_nin*

Blackorwhite

Jay Allisan is a lifelong daydreamer turned offbeat author, with a penchant for genre-hopping and a tendency toward the grim and the absurd. She primarily writes stories, most of which aren't true, and still wants to be Batman someday. *www.jayallisan.com*

Conveyor

Ciaran McCarthy is an Irish short story writer, currently based in Berlin. He graduated from Maynooth University. He spends a lot of time thinking about identity and existentialism, and enjoys reading and writing stories involving them. Occasionally, he can be found standing outside a field, talking to the cows. They have yet to reply.

Soon The Sentence Sign

David Hoenig is an academic surgeon who lives to write, instead of writing to live. He's had stories published with *Grim Dark Magazine*, *Flame Tree Publishing*, *Cast of Wonders*, and others. He has published a novel-told-through-verse-and-art with Oscillate Wildly Press, called "Queen To His King." He is (slowly) editing his first novel (sci fi). He's also a soul-gem carrying member of the HWA.

Bunny Racing

Tyler W. Kurt self-identifies as a teacher, writer, traveler, and trail runner. He practices law when bills come due. He has visited 55+ countries and has lived in Mozambique, China, and Argentina. Accordingly, he has learned and forgotten Portuguese, Chinese, and Spanish.

The Only Punishment

Ville V. Kokko is a Ph.D. student in Philosophy and an aspiring writer of both fiction and nonfiction living in Turku, Finland. So far, he has had several short stories and articles published in both English and Finnish. Some of his favorite topics to read and write about are philosophy, speculative fiction, and combinations of the two.

Human Contact

Frances Howard-Snyder teaches philosophy at Western Washington University but prefers to explore ideas through fiction. So, she was delighted to learn of a magazine seeking stories like The Trolley Problem. She is currently earning an MFA from the Rainier Writing Workshop and has published short stories in *The Magnolia Review*, *Halfway down the Stairs*, *Oxford Studies in the Philosophy of Religion*, and other places.

Additional Information

Reviews

If you enjoyed reading these stories, please consider doing an online review. It's only a few seconds of your time, but it is very important in continuing the series. Good reviews mean higher rankings. Higher rankings mean more sales and a greater ability to release stories.

Print Books

https://www.afterdinnerconversation.com

Purchase our growing collection of print anthologies, "Best of," and themed print book collections. Available from our website, online bookstores, and by order from your local bookstore.

Podcast Discussions/Audiobooks

https://www.afterdinnerconversation.com/podcastlinks

Listen to our podcast discussions and audiobooks of After Dinner Conversation short stories on Apple, Spotify, or wherever podcasts are played. Or, if you prefer, watch the podcasts on our YouTube channel or download the .mp3 file directly from our website.

Patreon

https://www.patreon.com/afterdinnerconversation

Get early access to short stories and ad-free podcasts. New supporters also get a free digital copy of the anthology *After Dinner Conversation– Season One*. Support us on Patreon!

Book Clubs/Classrooms

https://www.afterdinnerconversation.com/book-club-downloads

After Dinner Conversation supports book clubs! Receive free short stories for your book club to read and discuss!

Social

Connect with us on Facebook, YouTube, Instagram, TikTok, Substack, and Twitter.